HEDYPHAGETICA

HEDYPHAGETICA

A Romantic Argument

After certain Old Models, & Containing an
Assortment of Heroes, Scenes of Anthropo-
phagy & of Pathos, an Apology for Epicur-
ism, & Many Ojections raised against It,
Together with Reflexions upon the Bodies
politic & Individual, their Affections,
Nourishments &c.

by

AUSTRYN WAINHOUSE

Dalkey Archive Press
Champaign • London

First published in France by Collection Merlin, 1954.
Copyright © 1954 by Austryn Wainhouse

Library of Congress Cataloging-in-Publication Data

Wainhouse, Austryn.
    Hedyphagetica / Austryn Wainhouse. -- 1st U.S. ed.
        p. cm.
    ISBN-13: 978-1-56478-467-4 (alk. paper)
1. Political satire. I. Title.
    PS3573.A41215H43 2007
    813' .6--dc22
                            2006036443

This publication is partially supported by a grant from the Illinois Arts Council, a state
agency, and the University of Illinois, Urbana-Champaign.

Dalkey Archive Press
University of Illinois
605 E. Springfield
MC-475
Champaign, IL 61820

Dalkey Archive Press is a nonprofit organization whose mission is
to promote international cultural understanding and provide
a forum for dialogue for the literary arts.

www.dalkeyarchive.com

*Printed on permanent / durable acid-free paper and bound in the United States
of America.*

for Christopher Logue

Les sots sont ici-bas pour nos menus plaisirs.

Gresset.

OH MY, YES, I AM AFRAID THAT IN THE BEGINNING WAS THE WORD, THAT THE WORD WAS WITH GOD, that indeed the Word was God; afraid that there's no escaping it and its heavy consequences, for Him, for You, for Me. For the Word or more precisely the Noise that was in the beginning, or that lay waste the silence, substituting smouldering waste for silence, had inevitably to be doubled by another Eructation, the second one, a reply to the first and following long afterwards, likewise to be sounded with difficulty and at the end. After describing how and in what quantity and kind God fed when this first time He dined, He Who was even then His own aliment as He was His own cause, in seipso totus, teres, atque rotundus; after this description of His feast, the same exquisite old myth allows us to infer that the Noise—not, I repeat, meditated, but spontaneous and apparently accidental, not a terse statement, an authoritative command but, quite the contrary, a complaining wheeze started from untried and young bowels, a labored, a surprised, a painfully pushing grunt—must surely have been no less pathetic than it was obscene and thus also, fatally, necessarily, the act which succeeded it and creation generally. So, not merely out of thoughtlessness, oh my, no, but out of the most indicative weakness, so were wrought, so it would appear, heaven and earth,

the darkness quick writ upon the face of the deep,
the black waters in which the Maker's spirit roved
and the light that shew Him where it abode; so came
all that dwells on land, in the seas and aloft, licentious,
hungry, unclean, of base stuff, of imperfect line to be.
And when on the morrow the Lord God was sate,
gone out of rut or wine, or torpor or terror, done,
wiped, rested, returned to His sound senses and His
senses at ease, He looked, did He, and saw that it,
all this, was far, far from good, yea, He was ashamed
to behold what ruined vision and recoiling, drew a
mist over things in His image, that way to hide their
vicious organization, by hiding to pretend to modify
the unbearable unalterable, to abolish it through
ineffectual modesty, through vain remorse to atone
for it. Ah, He Who had never played the game
before, played it badly, bungling here, botching there,
it got Him nowhere and He shed at last a rain for
grief; His humiliation in this plight only fertilized
the clay which rose vengefully, like active yeast, exigent
and multiplying and thus, you observe, the foolish
abominable situation only worsened and all was lost
immediately there something was, irreparably and
mysteriously. Sterner measures, many vows, potent
remedies were needed, my dear, for confusion was in
the world, crime, sin, lust, a great packet of ill, it was
intolerable, unfitting and Who was God to support
hurt from the effect of His intemperance? the Almighty
rose up, magnificent and resolute, in high wrath tower-
ed He up and in despair, and He caught in trembling
fist this vast teeming excrement and bravely swallowed
down the universe entire, precisely, the world with
all its running, flying, wriggling, wobbling, swimming,
limping, offensive populations swallowed He them all

down, with a grimace thrust everything, bag and baggage, lock, stock and barrel into His accursing mouth whence this chaotic multitude of indigestible, angular, not easily to be reduced odds and ends descended into His belly, thence into His sublime entrails where, bless me, now it is, making slow troublous progress towards what we have not the slightest doubt, have we? These afflictions we know are grace-giving God's self-punishment, wise principle of justice; He is undergoing this in our behalf; fated later to emerge, perhaps soon to re-emerge, in an improved shape and of better substance, probably, the creation's second birth will be accompanied by the pronunciation of a Word, perhaps the same Word, or Noise, but this new time spoken or produced consciously and with decision; thus the legend concludes.

That, it seems to me, brings us down to the present, to this night, and to my present state of mind, my expectancy; how is it I am led to think on God and sympathize with Him more fully than ever I did before? Well, there is this taste of steel in my mouth and in my nose the anticipation of a gust of gunpowder's apocalyptic fartsmell.

Part the First:

OUR TOWN

And in my eyes, nothing. No, no tears in these dear old empty blear eyes of mine, weary from print and proof and more, and more. Not even the plan which came to me, surely came looking for me, for I go looking for no plans, not I, no longer. And even when stared at by a plan that would freeze another, I the no longer very fixable Lucius am not much to be had, nor loath, nor willing; but this plan I speak of lacked even what would be needed to arrest a child, and came timidly and I had no need to feign blindness, for it stayed a moment only, no more than a moment and was gone before I could murmur forfend, or raise my hand to my pen or my face. Apparently no eyes in my face, or if eyes, no hands on my stumps, hands perhaps, but indifferent ones, like the rest, if not stump-like then conditionless, believe me, conditionless, if you want to believe anything, if you can. You can if you please, Aimée, as can I who, even conditionless, still wish to believe somewhat: believe more or less at random now, the plan having vanished, and with much greater ease in this absolute mood or illusion, with this taste, with this smell whereunto I adverted a moment ago. I for example believe you when you say you are able to visualize me at twenty-five; something doubtless fills your keen bright eyes. Keen bright eyes! There it is, somewhere, apparent to you, hidden from me, that's the trouble, there's the manifest pity, there, in that deceitful distance which has undone what certainly must have been, as you say, my dear, beyond words agreeable, beautiful, desirable, which out of fairness to you I have got positively to declare has escaped me, at my age, and I it.

How far apart we have drifted. And must remain, I fear. I am afraid there are distinctions to be preserved, for once they've been attained after infinite striving, there's no being rid of them. Regret? I regret nothing, how could I? and that impossibility constrains me to offer a little of what they call resistance, I who am indeed in a precarious way and nigh to pure unconstraint. My little house would charm you. It has three storeys, the upper storey is a loft I have had turned into a study, the second storey has two bedrooms, one descends a delightful pine staircase, steep and narrow, to the ground floor which also has two rooms, a kitchen and a living room with of course a fireplace. The front door is of walnut strapped, hinged and bolted in old iron, the three steps are of worn old stone, the façade is brick. The street is not wide, nor long, nor straight, nor evenly paved, nor entirely; elms grow near the houses which are alike, not far away is a canal, a little further one comes upon another, there are numerous canals in Grön, as I suppose you know, and, communicating as they do with the river, one sees barges and boats in the canals whose water is still, indeed stagnant, indeed stinking, for ordures are dumped into the canals, leaves fall into them, so do papers and now and again people these days, why yes, it is no more uncommon to find expatriated or displaced or homeless people in the canals than it is, these days, to see a few of them on the street prone, inert or sparingly in motion, but only a few, and not many more pendent or solemnly sitting in the windows or standing in doorways, like signs. And what is a man if not a sign, wherever he be planted, however nailed or mounted, upon whatever commission, marking whatever borderlessness, a sign to look for, a sign which looks? and why should he not, if 'tis that which pleases him easily pleased by trifles, or if he be pleased to be nothing pleased in this nowhere, and bewildered dotes, why not, I ask, if he has a gentle nature and is patient?

These are the midtimes, the cleft twixt the good and the bad, the bad and the good times plentiful and lean, times when one is hard pressed to reckon how well or badly off one is, where the wind lies, if it blows, by what means or figures to do the little sums, when to sow or reap or eat or sleep or die, and how. I have my necessaries and the means to purchase some comforts, now and again a delight, though I know many of these are artificial needs. I have few cares, fewer today than yesterday, many less than a month ago; and carewise this has been a fine year, and needwise too, as a matter of fact. My health lasts; it will not be bone that will fail me, nor do I believe it will be nerve. As for my histories, they are esteemed suitably got up and useful, or were, when opinion used more to be arrived at than it is now; and I write less now. I believe I have been perfectly understood, or was at a time when there was more fuss and bother made over understanding, strange as all that may sound; but I fancy you know what I mean. And even now, even now, I dare say, I would be exceedingly well understood, conditions being what they are and being in the main rather unfavorable, but even so, even so I think I can declare that the little I accomplish enjoys an ample share of the limited amount of understanding committed and in circulation and however it may be limited it is not to be sneered at. And furthermore, Aimée, I have been and am yet aware of what I am doing—what do you think of that, my pet?—and these doings of mine stand me in excellent stead, I am, I say, aware of what I am about, of what it means, of who they are, of what they need, what I must give, where yield, and above all of the trend of diminishing meaning, needing, giving, yielding that gains headway as time and being pass on. On they pass, with more or less dignity and irresistibly, like the peaceful sun and stars, fading. I live peaceably in Grön; just as you predicted and counter to my immature fancies, the city is not yet utterly in pieces, great God no! it's moving to that end to be sure, but is still far from it: to a person well-advanced along the road Grön at the moment seems to be as solid as ever it was, and solider from that perspective. I am done judging its faults, or nearly done judging, as you required of me; Lucius has ceased to offer the world a scare. Salves are what they want, healing balm, my sweet, sugary preservatives, and that is what they get. Lucius is reputed very skillful at rectifications, smooth engraftments, neat establishments, but is no architect, not he. His is entirely a carpenter's trade, as it were: putting on varnish, scraping off paint, matching grain, shaping, hacking, hewing and trimming. But less of that now than formerly, quantitatively. It calls for a steady hand and no more than a minimum of invention— but the call is fainter. Find the scheme and materials to make good the end and trouble thyself for naught else, says he. Right, they reply. He says it less often, their reply is less prompt, less hearty. He has long

since conquered his distaste for the work; 'twas never
but prudish recalcitrance held him off; today he goes,
no, until late he went merrily to discorrupt and tran-
quillize readers to whom he has been bound by a
system, a law, a conscience (and yet is, but less firmly),
by a situation so entire, so exclusive as to eliminate
all possibility of choice, all idea of it... and now, would
you believe it? the idea creeps back, softly, subtly.
Would it be one of your high acts to slay it in slaughter?

Those scruples, those abrupt starts and quandaries
you, in a less formal period, correctly condemned
in him as being greatly out of place and more out of
season, that overcurious observance of decency, that
gigantine state of mind, were all quelled, suppressed.
All the knots and stounds in his head were worked
clear out; all those absurd notions and unpardonable
chastities were well wiped away; there was less to it
than he had dreamt: a little thrust, that sufficed; afterwards, not euphoria, but an epicurean reasonableness,
allow him to say it, a measured apathy immeasurably
richer than those ridiculous frights and squinting
hesitations. And now he is a result of his exercize,
the outcome of his discipline, and is rated for it by
his onetime mistress, like any honest woman ready
to see crimes here where echoes only resound if any
noise there is, ready to call the silence of his watchful
and serene habit a very false tone, very traitrous and
inhuman, ready to cry, Why does he not get himself
up? why does he not act? and to advocate a fresh policy.
She repents in her wooden friend's behalf. We shall
start out anew, she proposes, we shall reverse it all,
correct the mistake. There are after all other, loftier,

older considerations, and this she is able to write, not
to a boy, but to a man who, having for years done
nothing but delve in the past, knows very well what
it is, what it is good for. Aimée assures me she is
anxious and aggrieved, quite as if there were merit
in that, she says the light and warmth and the heart's
good cheer have fled far from her, and she enquires
whether, for Lucius' part, he is content. He answers
with some firmness that his cup doth overflow, declaring
it is a modest little vessel, but of a mighty capacity
withal, for its contents are pressed from a lucky vine.
It is a splendid June morning; nevertheless, it is bear-
able and all goes well, goes gradually and quietly.
He hears a volley of shots, ploop, ploop; ploop, ploop,
no, not leaden these shots, but as of dough falling upon
putty, shots wending their way along with nothing
like urgency through the elastic air and they melt
into the quiet, the well- and the gradually-going,
gently, casually consecrating the street's vacancy and
indicating that the Prince is elsewhere, in his tower,
his lady beside him, doped and happy, the Pricker
in his grave, the prisoner in his cell. He hears the
pad of rubber feet, four soldiers trot by, sunburned,
athletic, graceful in their loose-fitting costumes of
warm-weather lawn, four scantily attired young cham-
pions slobbering away from their pretty mouths;
they stop, drop to one knee, shoot, whinny and snigger
for the fun of it all and run off again, in step. Joy, eh?
A plane comes beckoned out of the west, buzzes at
the zenith, goes obediently east to crash, abandoning
the pure vault to Mercurius, spirit of communication,
genius of whoremongery, patron of letters; Lucius
has his pen between his fingers; no, in the whole sky
there's not a cloud as big as his hand then lo! he has

a communication from one who was his devoted mistress, who has now—now after twenty-three years—got to tell him men and the hour weigh evilly, icily upon her. That she is hungry, empty but of reproaches and the stone in her womb; and, says Aimée, how greatly otherwise was dear Lucius, her splendid animal of some time ago. Some time ago! Was he really otherwise? Is it worth denying? it seems plausible; yes, he dimly glimpses it for the truth, 'tis dim, but 'tis here. 'Tis a bother. Water, "terrible waters of time," she'd have him go wading in and splash like a child, thrash like a spaniel, upstream, downstream, yet a little further, further yet, look here, look there, look for something drowned, hunt for a corpse, for a mere bone, no, here, it's a fast-running stream, it's a broad one, now gets deep... these adventures are not to his taste. Was he otherwise? What does it cost him liberally to acknowledge it? What, when invited to a feast of scorn? No, my lovely one, it will not be settled, for Lucius has no recollection, his word upon it.

Nor need he warn you against counting upon the word given by a man—by that thoughtful and how ambulatory ephemeride, great and swift at change, nothing but departures and desertions—, on the word of a man who cannot, who will not remember, remember what he promised, that ever he could swear, or be bounden; trust me? Don't do it. I withdraw my phrase, strike it out, will strike them all out, for it doesn't matter, they don't exist, not really, I do not give you my word, dear Christ, I cannot give you what I have not got, what is nothing, I have nothing to give you, or exceedingly little; words fail me... no pity, hence no treachery. And no plan.

I have heard accused the shortness of memories. The complaint is just, is it not, and very idle. Be a philosopher. Sift it thus: memories are short, always, shorter still than foreknowing, and in vicious times, when the opinion of things is inverted and when of the truth there is prodigious contention and incertitude; when there's not a man, not one to be found anywhere about who is not distracted, moonstruck, and at least somewhat defiled; when the major part of life is narrowly and nakedly a business, and when overwhelmingly that business comes to getting pitch on others with more or less adeption, or having their money or wives to leave them clean; when the ruin of a name is a night's work, when the general case is desperate, destined thus to continue, no relief in sight, no sight, no desire to be relieved, and yet things aren't bad, not so bad, when the better way to make the best of the worst is by worsening it and thereby pleasing virtually everyone and winning a title or a prize; then is it not the wise dog who, like the one in the story, leaves off battling for the bone and eats the meat left on it?

Yes, old parables, quaint old sayings do provide comfort, don't they? Not that they can even in unlimited quantity really fill an empty head or stomach or whatever the aching cavity may be, but they are able to demonstrate the futility of these quandaries and hungers and needs; and, today, what a great help it is to have the futility of anything demonstrated. For, alas! I think we have all known two or three little disappointments, been now and again jostled, had some one time in our lives a modest little complaint if not a little criticism to offer; did you know that once upon a time a famous poet asked, But what does anything at all matter? However, that was long ago, much has happened since; but, dear oh dear, what can we do for our own gloom-ridden, they upon whose lips the music lies slain, out of whose heart the last knell has died, they whom, I think, know very little of the world, who, tempted by the world, deceived by temptation, finding no pleasure in deception, no joy in their fall, turn full of mortal sorrow and roll in anguish towards the wall?

Marivaux had me up and out of bed at seven. I got into my running togs and squeezed my grip-strengtheners for the customary quarter of an hour, then swallowed some coffee and reeled out of the house, down those worn old steps, up that crooked and pitted picturesque street. Thirty yards of this and I was panting. I cursed, it did me good. Then I glanced laterally at the dead gesticulating in the canal and I became frightened, the sweating began. I loathe those morning sprints, believe me, I do. On and on I went, knees pumping high in the intellectual style, my athletic supporter wringing wet and chilly and riding up my hot crotch, oh, it's disagreeable, my sharp elbows thumping my ribs, the hairs sticking to my perspiring legs, my flattened arches battered in my old sneakers, on and on. I have a galloping stride and used to be fast but now the pumping cuts down my speed. The route I am expected to follow takes me out to the rendering factory, then I lope home, smiling at tax-payers, if I encounter any, thumping my chest, if I can. They like their civil servants virile. A dew had fallen during the night, an early mist was yielding to the sun rising over the plain; it was already warm, the air was sweet, the weeds shone in the blasted lots. Clean flags were out. So were old women in black, clipping salads with their scissors, picking amidst the glass and junk, with their skinny little fists mashing down the dandelions in their sacks. They squinted at me as I passed, I smiled and waved. I saluted a flag or two. I don't much take to these exhibitions. I always return with cramped calves and a chafed crotch. But there you are: the bitter with the better; it's the artist's life, the life of the scholar, the author, cramped calves, a chafed crotch. There was a child. A little girl was squatting in the waste, she was digging a hole with a piece of a knife. I looked back over my shoulder— for when I run my head swivels— and saw her lift her filthy skirt, piss in the hole, stir with a finger. She was eight or nine, I'd say. I reached home in a rage.

I seemed also to have made it in good time. My man-servant was sitting in the living room, his feet propped on the fender, his collar unbuttoned, and he was reading a novel. "Why, sir," said he, "I didn't expect you back so soon. How did it go this morning?" Then he spat into the cold grate and said: "Oop-la. Pardon, sir."

It should not be true, Aimée, not at least wholly and unconditionally true to say that your letter sealed Marivaux' doom. Doom, eh? I suppose this is as good an opportunity as any I'll have to interject that I seem to find our language has lately got very inaccurate, that it is being made subject to every abuse, has indeed become abuse itself, has become a vehicle of error, has indeed assumed the carnation of error, of abomination at the present time when an execrable ignorance leagued with hunger puts many strange

words into vulgar mouths. Our myriad inane untaught chew all the shape out of our speech, grind the
sense away, suck up the essential juices, either spit out
a cracked, misshapen bruiting and lowing or, battening
upon signs, ingest their say, pass it down through their
entrails and irreverently eject it at the nether end,
changed absolutely; it's done without ceremony or
compunction and it's as nice as you please, for what
care they who are famished, save to be fed? They've
no respect for anything—the fact has been recognized
and turned to account—; words are become ordures:
that's the actual perspective. And as for doom—manipulated, instrumental doom—, it's everywhere about
the city, the solid irrefragable city, in the gutters,
the sewers, on pavements, you find it etched on walls,
the canals are freighted with doom, and all that despite
the calm. But this shocking state of affairs is not by
any means new. What's that? Do I hear you say my
attitude towards it falls somewhat short of serenity?
My attitude is perfectly official; it was the Accuser's
when thirty-nine years ago he pronounced his exordium,
and his emotion was just. There were thousands
upon thousands in their Sunday best, kneeling on
chalkmarks in the Place des Philosophes, properly
intimidated by the condemning stare, impaled by
the sustaining stare of Claude-Maxime and his military
entourage perched aboard tanks blocking the entrance
to the Cathedral; thousands of bright citizens tacked
to the guilty stones, you must remember it, you remember everything. "What is this infamous spirit
of yours? What is your buffoonery, your politeness,
your suave gibbering but a blasphemous horror? And
this attainted City? An obscene stew, a sump—noisy,
frivolous, licentious and unclean," the Accuser had

cried from within the Last Judgment portal. "I assure you: this exquisite civilization of yours is finished: crime was its dam, and our mission is to crush the infected monster she pupped." Those were his words. There had been a sigh, like a breeze, of awe, of blubbering, of relief. "O by the Wounds of Our Saviour," shouted that gallant soldier, "and His Infinite Mercy, before you all I do swear an end—" He had clapped his hands to his lips, those nearby had beheld him to shudder; several of his trenchmouth ulcers had burst; lieutenants had tears in their eyes too; bells were rung in the hôtel de ville's towers; airplanes flashed overhead. On the following day, pandemonium at the Bourse. Although most of the Nation was far from dissatisfied, there was talk of collapse; the régime was not three days old when the murmuring began; it originated in high places and filtered down into the low.

But to return to that man Marivaux. For my part I do not believe, if you wish to pretend to reason you cannot maintain, and I am convinced Marivaux would never dream of declaring, or even of supposing, that he is doomed; doomed? certainly not! what nonsense! what irresponsibility! He has been dismissed, retrenched, put out of the house after five years in it, and that arbitrarily, if you wish, despotically, call it what you will, let him make of it what he pleases... no, he's out, he's gone. He went without references, without a single statement attesting his good character and insofar as I can make out he has an exemplary character; but what exactly do I know? and upon what might I dare take oath? Swear to that? never. For how could I be certain? no, he went without separation pay or compensatory wages or indemnification or any pension or material consideration or any pros-

pects and it is safe to wager without any private funds,
for he did not expect this; how could he have expected
it? Yet, even had he had some intimation, I am
sure—for I know my Marivaux, better than you know
him and probably as well as he knows himself—, I
am sure he would not have made the customary provisions, for he was not the kind of man who stints
himself, or saves; I sent him packing, do you see,
and there was nothing whatever to say, no time to
bicker over a settlement or recriminate in the least.
I gave no reasons, I do not consider myself obliged
to explain my actions to a domestic, indeed, I had
no explanations worth developing for him—once
started, you will note, these things invariably lead far—,
and he did not ask me to put myself to visibly fruitless
trouble on his account. Perhaps, on the other hand,
he did see it coming, for he heard me coolly, without
flinching, but why? Go softly there. More dangerous speculations in which the temptation is all too
great to become mired down. He went quickly,
quietly, I have not the faintest notion to what fate
—but what authorizes you or me to fancy to a doom?
The thing is to be doubted; I discharged the man this
morning: are dooms arranged and undergone in a
day? Think nothing of the sort, dear Aimée; dooms
are long in the preparing and their experience is prolonged; whereas these pseudodooms you hear of and
are apt to see in the marketplace are chitty inexcus-
ably wrought-up phenomena, in the main just epi-
sodic, but how these accidents are cried up, my stars!
what they are wont to make of trifles! all flurry and
haste and intemperance, the end of the world, it's
come! shrieks malice, and a minute later the mediocrity is counterbalanced by something similar and

equally null, 'tis forgot, the general scheme is recti-
fied, the world goes on. Where was I? He went,
I repeat, and I am left here, that's where I am, without
a servant and in a delicate position.

Nevertheless, I do not blame you or your letter
for my actual inconvenience, although my decision
was far from taken independently of you or it. Marivaux' case had probably been pending, by which
I mean this was, from the looks of it, an old and intri-
cate affair: it must have begun long ago, perhaps
five years ago, and have been now evoked and reacti-
vated by certain contingencies, then suppressed and
suspended by others I might with greater justice call
exigencies; in all likelihood it teetered this way and
that, I fancy neither of us discerned all the throbbings
and for the greater part mild undulations, but they
were many, recurrent, and the business was bound
to turn out badly, for associations of this nature seldom
last, they pall early and wisdom counsels that they
be dissolved soon. More than usually tenuous, this
little affair wore on long past its season and may have
been dead prior to this morning, it may have perished
long ago, perhaps five years ago, and continued mum-
mified, or like an appearance lassitude holds over
in shipwreck. At any rate, very little was required
to bring that tiresome and mainly silent arbitration
to its issue. Then, paf! You are at liberty to describe my use of Marivaux as unfair and capricious.
I might have kept him on another five years, another
decade, I might, who knows? have continued to receive
the most ample satisfaction from him, all the clouds
might have drifted away after this excess of feeling,
all, oh yes, might have gone brilliantly between us,
a fair sky, no complaints, no suspicion; well, it is con-

ceivable, I admit, but improbable. Five years later, or five months or merely five days, I might have been in a position to bring the very gravest charges against this man: he could have been guilty of all sorts of indiscretion, disobedience, wastefulness, immorality, my God, who can tell? it were altogether possible he could have become an intolerable embarassment, a stone around my neck, a cross to bear, an ignominious brand, it were not unthinkable he might have contributed to my defamation, he might have robbed me, ruined me by any of a hundred various means, conspired against me or, moved by jealousy or vengeance or anything at all (for where the will exists it is not long in seeking justification for what it desires; if the desire be imperious, it will rapidly discover the way to gratification), he might have undertaken it is impossible to say what—and then, paf, you know. Well, people were beginning to talk; I have described their language. Who is able to say what could have happened? and who could have guaranteed me against what I may have spared myself by obeying an impulse? For it is no easy thing to fathom the mind or the heart of another, impossible to predict another's behaviour, folly to rely upon it's being good: what security exists in an ignorance no matter how well established? Why then, you will say, Aimée, one dares not cross the street for fear of being struck down. Quite so, Aimée, quite so, I reply, and do not think the less of me for staying safely at home once I have got through my morning exercizes. We are, all of us, naturally alone. And at this moment I am at home and alone and without a valet, for better or for worse, for better, I believe. True, the next man I take on, if I choose to renew the risk I necessarily run by exposing myself to a taken-on servant, may prove an assassin or a thief. But whatever I have done or may do, it is not against you I bear any particular grievance; we are virtually done with Marivaux, whom I mention because he brought me your letter.

It was he sauntered up to my library with your letter in his hand. I was, this morning, in a dreadful state, weary from that absurd running, perplexed and made melancholy by thoughts of failing youth and vigor sport is supposed to do something to retard, according to some advice, to correct; but in my case, it produces the opposite effect and no illusion whatsoever, and if there were any proof I needed of debility's approach, or onslaught, these tragic mornings provide it in abundance. It once occurred to an influential administrator that, historians dealing with the past and their effort being to bring back to life what is old, a little exercize ought to be the ideal preparation for a day of inspired work; this formula precipitated five or six others just as strange. However, weakened rather than bolstered by this reminder of what awaits the seasoned flesh, I fell to dreaming of tottering corporations, empires in collapse: if sober objective analysis is a virtue in an historian, expect nothing but vice from the one whose calligraphy sputters and shakes in the shadow of angina pectoris. The concrete cause bred abstract ones, the particular developed into the universal, thanks to a movement of sympathy, or a spasm of self-pity. I shall do my best to reconstruct it. Like my heart, my memory is also weak, as you know. The very obscurity of the incident and the confusion of my ideas... but I continue; I have learned how to stop when the last moment arrives, I have found out how it is done, but I haven't

the strength to do it now. Wait, wait a little. I was
at work, barely. I was doing, imperceptibly, little by
little, slowly.

I was at work. I was writing—no, that is false.
I was thinking of writing about the period of Grön's
antiquity, about our Roman origins, as a matter of
fact it seems to me I was meditating upon Aegillius'
rosiform circumvallation; I had before me the crucial
passage in which young Aegillius describes the military situation, his march north from Nîmes, his arrival
at the site of Grön, his distress at finding the city in
rubble. He announces to his uncle he has instituted
restorations and has built a wall in the form of a rose;
Aegillius adds: "...an innovation, Sextus Carus, dictat-
ed by our circumstances: we must anticipate assault
from either direction and that from within appears
the more to be redoubted." The remark unsettled
me. However preposterous may seem what I believe
were my feelings now that the mood has passed, they
were real enough then. I was disturbed to realize
that the purpose of the old ramparts was ambiguous;
and I was struck by the patently meretricious note
that rings through all of Aegillius' correspondence
with Caesar's deputy. The boy was a scoundrel.
And what patriot enjoys being forced to acknowledge
that the founder of his country was an idle fellow,
an untruthful, a scurrile creature? and then what becomes of the initial impulse, what of the motivating
principle? Even then, when they were so easy to come by
and so easily held, when they were light to support, best-
owed allure, in that time of graceful motions, was there
then no principle? were those stones laid in disgust,
casually, in no faith when faith was not onerous and
the blue sky no shame to love? I thought of the wall.

I think of it yet, but more calmly: all that is most important about that wall is irrecoverably sunk in an ocean of historic alluviations, blanketed and lost beneath countless layers of intrigue, lost in a chaos of many persons' self-seekings, their calculations, their contradictory acts; what remains is a tale of use and wear. Countless demolitions and re-edifications; a thorough unpurpose, so it seems, a thorough futility, that appears to be the truth and what could be more afflicting to an historian? what more sad? Which sadness, this morning, excited sentiments of nostalgia and loss, of regret, of keen remorse: which alone—not to speak of the withering shade of menace, of latent evil, the confusion produced by antagonists within and without, factions, armed divisions, greens and blues already, before Byzance was born, cloaked suborners, faithless friends, multiple defections and universal unsafety, the complicites between exterior and interior elements, danger everywhere, at every turn—was enough to cripple my own enterprise by draining away not only a basis but a reason for beginning or pursuing it further now it was begun. Thus, I suppose like Aegillius whose writings are also a tissue of fine apology, I faced a kind of emptiness unbounded by ramparts substantial or vestigial, I had not even an hallucination or two wherewith to be consoled: and thus I was naked, my heart palpitating. That depression has left me since, I only speak of it, believe it or not, to facilitate the intelligence of what I am relating somewhat against my will but out of complacency to you, my dear, to you. Yes, it's for you, for no other, and if this method of mine is distracting, what do you wish if not to be distracted? do I persist in this method for its own sake? Why no, I persist for yours. At the time, however,

I was scraping and scratching with a pencil, drawing fuzzy, irregular lines, bending them into circles, spirals, some faint, others dark and ragged, and I was doing all this in my own interest. My nerves were on edge, perhaps I had not eaten well or enough at breakfast, all the symptoms were present, it had become something physical... a column of derisive sunlight fell with almost sensible moment upon my desk, it was something almost solid, to be weighed, there was a brutal glare leaping from the page, heat or brilliance or anger or the blindness one of them caused, something exasperated me, I felt squeezed, harried and was in a sweat; then he came in, and he was done for.

The room where I work is small: he filled too much of it. According to his instructions, he came in treading softly, so as not to interrupt my thoughts. Well, that was a mistake, for I had no real thoughts, only disagreeable sensations whose prise I would to God have been delivered of, whether by sudden motions, noise, words, any kind of an abrupt disturbance of the fatal hegemony that was consolidating. And Marivaux failed me. He, as it were, consecrated the outrage, he allied himself, for a moment only, it is true, unwittingly, innocently, but effectively nonetheless with the enemy... I repeat, with the enemy. Could anything be clearer? he came slinking up behind me, the very incarnation of menace, hovered in the shadow thickened by the noon incandescence, and slipped your letter upon my desk. I made out your hand on the envelope. That was enough. "You are discharged out of my service," I said, trying to keep my mind on the business as I stared at the fiery barrage pouring out of the sky and in through my window, "you will oblige me by getting out of my house at once. Off with you," I continued, cursing the light. I have never held a favorable opinion of the sun.

There was a pause. I could imagine his head lolling upon one shoulder, his chin falling, the eyelids drooping to half hide his eyes, the looseness traveling through his spine; he used to think that by doing these things, by achieving this attitude he looked *cute*, who knows where he got that notion. "I wonder," he said dreamily, doubtless fancying I'd be melted by that tone, "I wonder... they say Mr Johnson—"

"Dr Johnson," I shouted.

"—Dr Johnson will be coming out soon."

"Well, then you haven't a moment to lose," I said, perhaps a little cruelly, perhaps not, for Marivaux' distinction did not lie in his wit. "Go."

"Yes, sir," was his reply. That was all. He certainly grasped that without difficulty, and so must you. And you must believe me—rather, you, charming Aimée, might just as well believe me when I say that for a moment I knew the keenest anguish, a dread that penetrated into the deepest part of me. The crisis passed... I am less a sensualist than you may think... but oh, for a brief instant... you have no idea, I was nigh to unconsciousness... and then I recovered control of myself and for a space voluptuated in that cascade of detestable light; then rose, left your letter unread, and left the house, bewildered, only one clear thought in my head: that if I were to avoid being late for my dinner engagement I should have to hurry. There was black crape everywhere. My route took me through the market of St Henri-le-sale.

That market is not, these days, the most attractive or most wholesome place in Grön although it has come to be thought of as another of our national monuments; one wonders whether it were not far more gay and in a sense more picturesque if less monumental when, years ago, flowergirls hawked bouquets gathered in the country, sold flowers at St Henri-le-sale, when the country was other than it is now. But it is only treacherous sentiment, baleful sentiment which resists change and in its brooding lays a murrain curse upon the future by rejecting the present for barren. To the quick spirit and lively intellect, there are all sorts of fecundity, and what we have raised up out of a champain run to dry grey dust is perhaps richer and more ripe than what is suggested by the spectacle of peasants leading in cartloads of vegetables and fruits. Merchants caparisoning their wares with tulips and lilies, gypsies up from Spain, singers from the Marches, Provençal story-tellers, grinders, weavers, potters, with their wheels, their braziers, their looms and stuffs and clays and jars of glaze and lacquer, farriers with their iron straps, fishmongers in wooden clogs and brandishing awful knives, laughing, selling their carp and bream, loach, steel-blue eels, skates, shrimp and mussels, live terrapin and lobster and sleek trout, with lemons heaped high, with seashells, conches, mysterious green weeds festooning; much chaffer, higgling and raillery, much noise there must have been under the great sagging shed, within the intense odors and dusty sunbeams. However, all that's of the past, and thank God, I say, confusion is not now what we want. They've given up selling victuals in St Henri, but commerce goes on; today it's weapons, munitions, trophies. Cast off, not very brave stuff, rubbish most of it; 'tis all hardware, unglamorous, I grant you, but material and therefore reassuring, in a certain sense: handgrenades, obsolete guns, pistols broken-gripped or lead-plugged in the barrel, or with missing parts, triggers, springs, chambers, whatnot, cartridge cases for the mantel-piece and for widows' hairpins, medals for the idiot uncle or maid, citations, ribandery and whisky-stained polychrome silk collar- and chest-sized sashes, casques of all sizes for over the door or under the bed, trench-spades, pikes, picks, iron tent-pegs rusted to the dimensions of ten-penny nails, all objects prized by amateurs and connoisseurs, all kinds of oddments and warlike tokens, shrunken heads, hair and teeth, souvenirs of the East. The shed is still, our epoch has laid a hush beneath it, trade is minimized, negotiations are carried out with measure and dignity; out-sized blanket-pins, buttons, leggings, aluminum devices for swimming under water, aluminum combs, unoxidizable, fogged telescopic sights, goggles, waterproof dittie bags, bombs, fins and fuses and detonators for bombs, shells, little rockets, many tubes, inexpensive, usually aquatinted photographs of military heroes, the great thing about it is that none of it is controversial. A species of prostitution is also practiced here, against this setting one discovers a luxurious traffickery; assignations are concluded, it's the rendez-vous of Europe's most notorious sodomists and their agents, a serious, restrained set exhaling a sense of social position. I noticed the Orator of Venice in his wheelchair, a man of seventy years, soft-spoken, bright-eyed, elegantly attired, debilitated beneath his creams and paints; his male nurse was giving him injections. The Roumanian pretender's initiatrice was on hand with her two attorneys and a notary who was recording her transactions in a small notebook covered with mouseskin. Two grey-eyed English peers, young men with silver hair and pale complexions, had recently been witness to a hanging and it was of this they were comparing impressions. Scouts, thieves, buyers, soldiers slipped through the whispering, busy but orderly crowd and all would have gone with perfect smoothness had it not been for one of your wretched doom-criers come to affright the company.

A blind man vending theological tracts, a person directly out of a romantic novel, thrashed about with his cane, his bony jaw upraised, his blue lips drawn back, stretched like rubber bands over his gums; he snarled, he snapped at the air like some animal caught in a snare, he was bawling doom. "La jeunesse passe," he declared, advancing doom-howling upon the English gentlemen who had got their hands on an Arab child. The lords and the boy retreated, the foaming prophet staggered after, his eyes rolled white and weeping, sweeping, striking, denouncing the age's corruption, to avoid which the desert child skipped away, ducked nimbly into the glistening sunlight, grinning, and, but what would you expect? he was flung about ten meters by a vehicle, then crushed by a bulletproof tire and engulfed beneath what I fancied to be an armored bonnet. Doom, continued the enthusiast, and I am by no means loath to admit he was not entirely wrong; no indeed; it is simply a matter of emphasis and opportunity. The peers were manifestly annoyed—this melodrama was not to their taste—, they held a colloquy with the driver; not that they had anything pressing to say to him, not that they were the sort to strike up casual conversations with chauffeurs; but they turned almost instinctively in his direction, simply because, I suppose, the

39

driver stood in one place and the blind man in another, opposite him, and simply because, they probably felt, the blind man merited a scolding if indeed he were to be spoken to at all. The driver, himself irritated and taking umbrage before an unfamiliar accent, misinterpreted the impulse and instead of sheltering the Anglo-Saxons and making common cause with them, fell to defending himself by attacking the foreigners who, he might well have thought, intended to compromise him. "What," he demanded with great earnestness, "what in God's name do you expect?" One of the gentlemen replied unavailingly, in a lisp, the other urged calm; it was a tense moment; but the imperturbable, common sense of the English couple allowed them to master the situation and to assume leadership of the dialogue, although the blind man was virtually on their heels, nay, upon their backs, energetically crying his dark criticisms and constantly threatening to submerge liberal rationalism beneath a deluge of popular mysticism, its age-old and most mortal antagonist; and the latter would surely have carried the day had the Englishmen not resorted to a clever expedient: between the hoarse gasps of doom's creature they deftly inserted their opinions, which were chiefly modulative, not really expository, and supple. "No," said they as one man, "for it were useless to pretend otherwise." "But," interrupted the driver in his gleaming puttees, "this is the twentieth century, the twentieth—" Unfortunate iteration: it shattered the mold, disturbed the rhythm: when the two opened their pink mouths to express qualified assent, Doom exploded in the air; and the two looked at each other and smiled, tingling with the happiness that is born of a fair failure. Their relief was no greater

than my own; at last, I thought, at last. Even though
I knew, at bottom, it was not the last. It was, still,
like a glimpse of freedom. I continued along my way;
there was a buoyancy in my step, a cheerfulness returned to my heart, certain pressures had receded, certain
imperatives had been assuaged. It was time to eat.

Samuel Johnson, his parents' only child, heir to a
distinguished name and fortune of sixty thousand
obols a year, was born in Grön. His mother, a Guesclin,
died while giving birth to him; within the space of a
few months his father, municipal archivist under the
Republic, followed her into the grave. Samuel was
entrusted to the care of three prosperous bachelor
uncles: Valerian, Julian and Adrian, persons likewise
of condition upon all of whom was stamped the elegant
Johnson look: they were long in the face, silver mous-
tached, had tanned skin, black eyes, high foreheads,
tall, lean figures; in a word, something of the old
Spanish aspect; they were frequently voyaging, widely
experienced and acquainted, gallant, subtle, witty
and chill. Valerian was a financier, Julian a manufacturer, Adrian dealt in international trade: all three
gentlemen were powerful, influential, belonged, it
may be conjectured, to certain select fraternities and
clubs and, needless to say, to the conservative minority
of which they were reckoned to be very pillars; by an
incongruity visible to those, especially modern, eyes
which avidly discover paradoxes everywhere, they
were also liberal, but liberal in a sense that has ceased
commonly to be accepted by a generation that retires
at ten and which, even in their day, had already begun

to be the source of anguished misunderstanding and repressive legislation; to avoid whose effects, these fastidious personages observed a strict silence about their affairs and kept their opinions to themselves for, even in their day, opinion, like passion, had lost considerable ground with not only the administration but the public and had become something which could have only a well masked existence. Thus, little Johnson was brought up in surroundings which had inevitably to turn him into an outlaw. Now here was an unusual case. That he was of a mild and sweet and peaceable spirit was not enough; his first, those most important, impressions were received in what may only be described as a kind of exquisite clandestinité in which there were midnight comings and goings, curious rules and rituals, furtive signalings, arcane winks, nods and handclasps, an entire underground paraphernalia. By the time he attained his twenty-first year, these men, upon whom Samuel relied for guidance and example and to whom he was attached not merely by ties of consanguinity but by those necessity forges between a conspirator and his fellow-plotters, these men, I say, were dead, and Samuel was left to wage the battle alone.

From the beginning Johnson seemed to incline towards the sciences; needless to say, those he preferred were occult; he also took pleasure in solitude and exhibited unmistakable signs of becoming a great eater. The little boy developed a quiet, even disposition, much self-control; there was something of the intrepid in his character, although nothing of the desperate; his expression was grave and watchful, he seldom laughed, spoke little, he was shy. However, what he did say was clearly pronounced; no infantile burbling, no stammered nonsense came out of his mouth; he was intelligent and indeed wise beyond his years and because of his truly ravenous appetite he grew quickly. For teachers he had his uncles and the masters they hired to train him in the mechanical skills; but it was from Valerian, in whose magnificent town-house he lived, and from Julian and Adrian, with whom he had weekly appointments, that he received the most valuable instruction. The three men, each proprietor of a veritable fortress, were mainly concerned to teach him how to sustain what they termed the *siège*. His early, virtually recluse years were uneventful, the curriculum he was given was broad, the standards he was expected to meet were rigorous; careful planning and much expense were lavished upon his upbringing and his guardians proudly felt they and he could be congratulated upon the favorable results which were announced almost at the outset. But because the scholar and his uncles were none of them of an expansive turn, rather sober in the extreme and incapable of abrupt displacements, their intercourse was as formal as their deportment was austere. Barring a few superficial details, this was close kin to the life of the camp.

There came the day when Samuel, now a lad of fifteen, begged to know what Valerian supposed his nephew ought to become.

"Become?"

"Yes, Uncle," said Samuel, "what must I do?"

The banker said: "There is either doing or refraining from doing—I visualize those alternatives. Consider the fashion in which the matter is taken up by Plato," Valerian continued, darting a glance at the sturdy oak-paneled door, at the twice-grilled windows. "There is either the passive or the active life. You will recollect *Republic*, Steph. II, p. 496. Socrates and a sophist, whose identity and argument are surely familiar to you, debated which of the two more promoted the cultivation of virtue, a condition which was, in that epoch (allow me to remind you), associated with happiness, which in turn was intimately related to duty. Socrates placed felicity in an equal and constant state of mind and the sophist in much desiring and much enjoying. The sophist declared Socrates' felicity was that of a block of stone. Socrates replied that the sophist's felicity was the felicity of one that had the itch, who did nothing but itch and scratch. Have you raised the question before your other uncles?"

Samuel approached Julian. "Do?" asked the manufacturer, narrowing his eyes, frowning, compressing his lips, "do? Above all else, I should advocate caution."

"Caution, Uncle?"

"Exactly. Caution, to cite one of your favorite renaissance apologists, is when men ingeniously and discreetly avoid to be put into those things for which they are not proper: whereas, contrariwise, bold and unquiet spirits will thrust themselves into matters without difference, and so publish and proclaim all their wants. Our own period is heavily charged with instances of what occurs when one acts in plain defiance or in ignorance of these principles; but rather than fatigue your young mind with a host of dreary examples of what is done contemporarily, I should instead prefer to illustrate the thing by a parable I take out of one of England's wisest clerics. He tells of how the lion called the sheep to ask her if his breath smelled. She said aye; he bit off her head for a fool. He called the wolf, and asked him. He said no; he tore him to pieces for a flatterer. At last he called the fox and asked him; truly he had got a cold and could not smell." Julian bade Samuel good night.

"I can only repeat to you what my brothers, who are of my own mind, have already said," declared Adrian to whom Samuel addressed himself next. "I think you ought to consider how the constitution of your nature sorts with the general state of the times; which if you should find agreeable and fit, then in all things give yourself more scope and liberty; but if differing and dissonant, then in the whole course of your life be more close, retired, and reserved. To be brief, look inquiringly about."

The three brothers met for dinner at Julian's home; Samuel was there too and after discussing the war, the cost, the folly, and smiling tolerantly upon the sin, the armaments purveyors' conversation soon came round to the problem of what the youth should become, what he should do. "A much maligned but singularly perceptive and indefatiguable moralist has gone to great lengths to demonstrate a doctrine which holds that because in the universe all is in movement, nothing at rest, everything and everyone must infallibly act, motion being the soul of the cosmological economy, repetition its form; according to this same writer, mankind is divided into those individuals who act badly and those others who act well, who are evil and who are good, that is to say, destructive and beneficient, it being assumed for the sake of the argument that to create is to do well, a notion which yet lingers here and there amongst us. That it is better because more advantageous to be vicious than virtuous, that the good are forever weak and victimized by the wicked who are mighty and invincible, these are interesting hypotheses

I will not strive to discredit. In your later years you will be able to explore them at your leisure and with the thoroughness they deserve; but for the time being it is enough to point out that this man is clearly right when he affirms that so long as the general interest of mankind drives it to corruption, he who does not wish to be corrupted with the rest will therefore be fighting against the general interest. Do not, Samuel, do your utmost not to find yourself in that awkward posture," Julian warned, giving his nephew's arm an affectionate squeeze.

"That doctrine," said Valerian, "is not without its perils, for its triumphant application expects a fine discrimination in order justly to appraise the drift of things or ceaseless agitation in order to impose a direction upon them; one need but be lacking in the one or fail at the other and ruin is the almost certain consequence. Yet if to the casual glance that system appears rude and malevolent—or pessimistic or cruel—, notice how it compares with the allegedly very mild, very humane, very sagacious counsel a Chinese philosopher, who was also a politician, gave his disciples. Be trustworthy in every respect, said Confucius, starting in a more hopeful vein; be devoted to the acquisition of learning, steadfast unto death for the Good. But what does that Good now prove to be? Do not, the master goes on, do not enter any area which is running dangerous risks, nor live in one where the people are in rebellion. If the Way prevails among the states, you can make yourselves prominent; but if it does not prevail, then keep in retirement. If it prevails in your area, it is a disgrace to be poor and humble. If it does not prevail, it is a disgrace to be rich and honored." Valerian paused, then, in response to what he took to be a shadow of disconcertion that had come across the boy's face, promised they would return to the Way at some future date. "The crux of the matter seems, does it not, to lie in that mysterious concept. My advice is to wait."

Julian glanced at Valerian, Valerian regarded Adrian, Adrian peered at Julian, then the three men stared at Samuel who, rather than demanding to know to what end he should take all these precautionary measures, accepted to wait, lowered his eyes, and held his peace.

Johnson was sixteen when upon that unforgettable 17th of July Claude-Maxime achieved his effortless coup d'état and, upon the 18th, summoned the Grönards to assemble at the Place des Philosophes. What a stirring sight it had been! what a moving speech! The day had been fair and warm, the crowd vast and receptive. Samuel had been pressed against a woman of perhaps thirty-five or thirty-eight, who wept uninterruptedly throughout the ceremony. It lasted a full two hours during which that great collection of bourgeois became progressively more and more aroused, more and more ecstatic and finally gave way altogether when the oath of purity, loyalty and credulity was administered. Cries, quavering hurrahs burst forth, they clapped their hands, shuffled their feet, some smiled, others sobbed. "The end of an era!" "The beginning of a new one!"

"What do you fancy it means?" Samuel asked, casting alarmed glances in every direction.

"Oh, dear, dear little boy!" exclaimed that lady at his right. She threw her arms about young Samuel, kissed his cheek, his brow, his ear, his neck, his lips, it was useless to resist, he opened his mouth to complain, their tongues entwined. Squeezed in by his neighbors, he could not escape her embrace or defend himself against her hands, her legs, her whole body; she had shut her eyes, she was deaf to his whispered protests, his supplications, insensible to his thrusts and pushes or all too eager to misinterpret them. But this had not prevented Samuel from seeing it all.

The Accuser had terminated his inflammatory speech, had clapped his hands to his mouth, those near him had rushed to his aid, the throng had got to its feet and rushed to leave the square by the narrow streets which radiate out from it. Thanks to the crush and his companion's firm grip, Samuel had been carried along with this woman who requested him to call her Beatrice. They had been precipitated down a dark passageway, then down another and a third; Samuel had lost his bearings. "Come," said the lady, "poor boy, I will give you refuge. Come with me," and she led him through courtyards and gardens and buildings and down stairs, her hand always locked upon his wrist. It was a labyrinth they traversed—the faint, troubled light that sank wearily down airshafts, as something feeble enquiring in an ocean of despair, the sweet, moist odor of tiny ruelles, the depressing atmosphere of vaults, of corridors, of tunnels, of condemned buildings... they arrived before a door. To the boy's distracted glance it seemed thin.

"I don't see how—" Samuel began. "Oh yes, you will be safe here," Beatrice said in her queer voice, urging Samuel to enter an apartment filled with Empire furniture, with a piano run by a motor, with an immense porcelain-bricked stove, with couches that seemed damp. The walls were covered with stained orange paper in turn hidden, or further spotted, by drawings of actresses, photographs of dancers. The untidy little nest was lit by dim electric lamps shaded with taffeta; frills, lace, India prints, leather ottomans, books, papers, bottles, pillows, clothing and many other things lay strewn everywhere. Confronted by an impossible intimacy, Samuel was again assailed by a wave of sadness; he gasped, he felt stifled, he sought to flee; he was checked by a thigh and a plump little belly, like a blister. The door closed. "Ah. Poor dear boy," said Beatrice, lifting her chin, a look of strange pride and seriousness fixing upon her thin face. Samuel missed his dinner.

It amounted to a breach of discipline, an infraction of the security code. "This is unprecedented," said Valerian; "I must have an explanation." Samuel attempted to give him one. "You have spent the afternoon with a woman?" "Perforce."

"You will not think it indiscreet of me to ask what woman?"

"Beatrice." "Beatrice." "The most unpleasant of women." Samuel touched his finger to his temple. "I came to some dreadful conclusions."

"Ha. I see." Valerian modified his tone. And then, as one of the besieged to another: "But sit down, Samuel." "Thank you, Uncle." "What is it, old man? You don't look well." Valerian called for armagnac and one glass. "Compose yourself. Are you hungry?"

"Yes," said Samuel; "this has come as a shock."

"Of course. Of course." Valerian called for an omelette, sandwiches, wine, fruit. "So it went badly? You are not compromised?" Food was brought in. "Your honor?..." "No, no, hardly," said Samuel, devouring the eggs. He seemed to be sniffing the air,

4

49

his eyes darted left and right, he appeared to be worried. "I have a few questions, Uncle."

"You may be sure I am entirely at your service. But might it not be merely a matter of how to conduct oneself in love? For in that case I should be able to furnish the approved formula in extenso. It dates from the twelfth century and our present author is Andreas Capellanus, who opens with the following little prologomena (chew your food, Samuel, and endeavor to pay close attention): Love is a certain inborn suffering derived from the sight of and excessive meditation upon the beauty of the opposite sex, which causes each one to wish above all things the embraces of the other and by common desire to carry out all of love's precepts in the other's embraces." "That's it," said Samuel, whose expression could not have been more downcast.

"Then Andreas proceeds to dilate upon his subject and in an orderly manner lists the rules which govern amorous commerce among the high-bred. First he speaks of marriage which, says he, is no real excuse for not loving. Next, he who is jealous cannot love. No one can be bound by a double love. It is well known that love is always increasing or decreasing. That which a lover takes against the will of his beloved has no relish. This is sound stuff."

"Yes," Samuel observed. His eyes were hollow, his cheeks pale. "Go on, Uncle."

"Sixthly" —Valerian's voice resounded in the granite-bound room—"boys do not love until they arrive at the age of maturity." Samuel's expression was grim. "When one lover dies, a widowhood of two years is required of the survivor. No one should be deprived of love without the very best of reasons." Samuel emitted a low noise, like a little growl. And emitted another as Valerian pronounced: "No one can love unless he is impelled by the persuasion of love. Love is always a stranger in the home of avarice. It is not proper to love any woman whom one would be ashamed to seek to marry. A true lover does not desire to embrace in love anyone except his beloved. When made public, love rarely endures. The easy attainment of love makes it of little value; difficulty of attainment makes it prized. Every lover regularly turns pale in the presence of his beloved. When a lover suddenly catches sight of his beloved his heart palpitates. A new love puts to flight an old one. Good character alone makes any man worthy of love. If love diminishes, it quickly fails and rarely revives. A man in love is always apprehensive. Real jealousy always increases the feelings of love. Jealousy, and therefore love, are increased when one suspects his beloved. He whom the thought of love vexes eats and sleeps very little. Every act of a lover ends in the thought of his beloved. A true lover considers nothing good except what he thinks will please his beloved. Love can deny nothing to love. A lover can never have enough of the solaces of his beloved. A slight presumption causes a lover to suspect his beloved. A man who is vexed by too much passion usually does not love. The thirtieth article, my boy, is this: A true lover is constantly and without intermission possessed by the thought of his beloved. And the last: Nothing forbids one woman being loved by two men or one man by two women. Well," Valerian concluded, "what do you think of it?"

"I wonder," Samuel answered, "whether I shall not be the last of my line."

"Have you had enough to eat?"

Samuel remained silent, did not seem to have heard, did indeed seem to be listening, but for something far away and out of earshot. The silence was made precise and bright by the meter of stone that defended without seeming to constrict the room. His slender hands resting patiently on his knees, Valerian rang and with a smile at once ironic and tenderly speculative watched a domestic carry the dishes away, whisk away the crumbs; the smile departed, a look of mild concern took its place, and the gentleman turned questioningly towards his nephew who, scarcely breathing, the color returned to his cheeks, his eyes shining with something that approached fever, listened, failed to hear, but nevertheless felt he could sense that ending of an era, or imagine it: the fireworks, the bunched flags, salutes and drums and heat, the feasts, the drink, drunkenness, vertigo, dryness.

It was accompanied by a terrific wave of heat, of thirst. That docile, incomparably patient population grew restless. Men of means, in their carefully brushed dark suits, furled umbrellas or dispatch-cases beneath their fleshy arms, black Homburgs plumb crowning crimson, would draw timepieces from their waistcoats and weep softly, while waiting in ante-chambers or for the news. The street-porter lost his way, then ceased to bear the load; little girls went bad. There were smoking yellow days and damp suffocating nights which seemed to rot the flesh in which the sun had slain all vigor, disoriented the will. The brothels were deserted. The diplomats had left for home. Cockfights, bearbaitings, open-air wrestling bouts featuring greased women did, it is true, draw large crowds, but they looked on absently, their faces puzzled, breathing with difficulty, licking their dry lips, squinting.

Manufacture, trade effectively halted; the industrial-
ists and the shopkeepers eyed the trend, the sag,
hesitated and preferred to watch and wait and sit in
the cool dark behind unfurled iron. Currency inflated,
currency reforms, decrees, arrests and a few disposses-
sions ensued: it did very little or only temporary good,
then the slump again, afterwards the indifference,
constantly the loss. They asked themselves whether
they had not had enough; but hadn't, not yet, stuck,
were ruined, they swore, couples slept apart, legs wrapped around bolsters or pillows, fumed and swore.
The war groped sullenly ahead, too remote, too uncertain to beget attitudes or arouse discussion; nothing
was discussed; the troubles, debts, listlessness increased,
nothing checked them, they bit their lips, their nails,
edifices tumbled until indeed the terrain looked clearer.
Things appeared to have attained a standstill only
the weather made grievous; perhaps this immobili-
zation would have been welcome had circumstances
been other than they were, had the stillness been pure;
perhaps, who knows, this was the secret impulse, this
impurity may have been what provoked the anguish
no one could identify or explain; it may have been
because of a yearning unfulfilled, not simply because
of the raging, petrifying heat, that the people fled
the staleness and infection of their homes and fled
into the streets to catch the breath of fresh night air
dream. Fights broke out among the idle, vanished
as the idle fell inert; public monuments were disfi-
gured; a dolorous obscene quality became general
and had perplexing, contradictory effects. It hovered
like fear or significant error in the atmosphere, it
discolored objects, staining them, like plaster sweated
through by humidity, that suffused plaster upon those

decaying fabulous walls which, they say, is one of the unmistakable features of old sinful cities. Haggard expressions wrote over faces blotched scarlet by the sun's heavy blows; then the tongue lost the power, or the desire, to taste, the eye to discern, bodies precisely to sense, the nerves to speak, voices became faint and white, it was just possible to hear the cats screaming through the city without milk. The smells began and were not really noticed until after they had become terrifyingly sweet; yet no one seemed genuinely terrified; which gave one the impression the power to be terrified had become suspended. And that was a blessing. Water ran short. It did not seem greatly to matter. There were fires at night. They were extinguished, or they burned. Trees and plants withered in the public gardens, along the boulevards. Men stood motionless, where they were, or staggered, or scratched, or stared, or shut their eyes against the brutal light, or painfully opened blood-shot eyes, the blood risen to their heads, or abandoned themselves, aimlessly, foolishly, to brutal acts wherein they took no joy, whereby they were little deceived, wherefrom they gained no confidence, which was one great thing they lacked, but did not seem to want, or miss, wanting, missing meant less than before, nothing at all. Most of them were too deeply within it, unable to observe. Although it was prolonged, intense, everywhere and conspicuously about, almost all failed to realize that history in this exaggerated, nightmarish form is nothing other than a shared, hence banal, interior experience, fugitive because infinite in extent, not something one is truly in, but something which is in one. And that is why I say this hallucinating transitional hour might have lasted forever. But in early September people woke to learn to their secret dismay that the crisis was over, ended, as it had been begun, by decree; the news was not discussed. Not, no, that things had returned to normal, to what previously they had been. There are no restorations. In time, people had grown accustomed to that invasion they perceived as immersion—to what the nervous, zealous young men who composed excessively detailed statements could not bring themselves to describe merely as new. Official language and zealous young men had not been able to. That they had not aroused no discussion.

Entrenched, so to speak, in their several retreats, Johnson's uncles, highly skeptical and not a little worried over personal losses amounting to millions, had followed developments with the keenest attention, and the boy had partaken of their interest: he had only an imperfect understanding of what was afoot and surely for that reason the more eagerly scanned its manifestations. He made an important discovery. The threat was twofold. There was not simply the danger of being crushed by the besieging outside world with which one had to reckon; that danger, huge and harrowing as it was, seemed, indeed, as nothing in comparison with the other, which he was now beginning to mark: the world's monstrous instability. It seemed, by all evidence, to be gripped by an urge to be undone, to decompose, be gone, but not according to a natural process or for natural causes the reason could grasp. Rather, the world seemed like a great idiotic half-tamed beast, half-conscious; there was something wrong with it, it was sick, at the mercy of a kind of aching shame, borrowed but self-imposed and which unceasingly urged it towards gradual destruction, that progress being just as unceasingly interrupted by

grotesque whinings, tricks, tremblings, fits of self-pity.
Plainly incurable, this wretchedness was the most
terrible weapon of all: its effect could be likened to
the power the suicide holds over those surrounding
him, those who, although his enemies, and above all
if they are his enemies, must care provided they care
for themselves: and so its effect was also to spread the
contagion of despair, to cause or tempt the besieged
to cease to care for themselves, to communicate that
unspeakable dark stubborn sadness which annihilates
integrity, assimilates all it touches into an eternal night
of disgrace. Samuel could do no better than glimpse
the problem in its bolder outlines.

"What horrifying ugliness!" he whispered, peering
out through the bars. "But surely," he added at once,
"it can't be as bad as all that."

No, the brothers were not hurled into bankruptcy
after all. They had financed and supplied at least
fourteen large and small wars. Such men cannot
fail. And sure enough, an obscure aggressor took to
the field in the nick of time. But Samuel was taken ill.
He suffered from periodic vomitings and an unrelenting
migraine. At night, in his delirium, he would speak
about eating and especially *the mouth*.

They, the four of them, went to St Luc and spent
a fortnight at the seashore. Samuel's vomitings stopped little by little; his obsession with the mouth did
not, and his migraine worsened. He was brought
back to Grön; physicians were consulted; not a moment
to spare, they said, and operated. His right eye was
removed, impairing his looks.

Valerian sat by his bed. He was dressed in grey
flannel, had come carrying an umbrella, wearing
a Homburg hat, the tips of a snowy white handkerchief

showed above his pocket; the room was obscure; he seemed almost not to be there.

"They didn't have to do that," Samuel cried as soon as that grey blurr offered proof it was Valerian. The boy's voice quavered with rage and disgust, he repeated: "They were not obliged to take it out. Why did they?"

"I don't know, my boy," Valerian replied softly, but not very convincingly.

Samuel stared at himself in a mirror. It was hard to see, there was not much to see. But all the same: "What ugliness!" he exclaimed, gasping. "What horrifying ugliness."

Valerian seemed less and less to be there.

Valerian died somewhat later. Samuel went down and turned his one eye upon the corpse. He bent stiffly and for a moment touched his cheek to the dead man's. Samuel went out. Time passed.

He showed Adrian a letter he had received; the spaces between printed words contained barely legible abbreviations, ornate and numerous, written in ink and with a pen so fine and, it seemed, so unsteadily guided the effect was of a broken spiderweb, a snarl of hairthin wire. "What do you make of it?" he asked. Adrian was ill. "Obey instructions," he said after Samuel had enquired whether in his uncle's judgment there might not have been a mistake.

But no, not at all. The recruiting station was indeed located in a church, in the transept, below a stained glass window: three dusty tables, three splintery chairs, three derelict non-commissioned officers in the scented air and difficult light: two invalided corporals, as if spellbound, their eyes vacant, rapt, and a sergeant who, meticulously, ceremoniously, moved one of his nickel-steel hands, made whorls and loops, each of which was spoiled by a squeak of hinge, by a spatter of ink that sprayed like mist over the drawn thread. The chin and jaw of one of the corporals had been shot away. "We've all been through a lot," the sergeant said. A group of women in black led by a priest trod past, holding lit candles, filing towards the altar. "We're buddies," the sergeant continued, "always together."

"That must be nice," Samuel said. A twittered *te deum* began, abruptly ceased; coughs from the depths of the church; the sound of coins falling on coins in one of the boxes.

"Been together a long time, in fair weather and foul, a lot of that, a lot of combat, but that's not always the worst. There's sitting around too, you know." "I know." "That one, the one looks all right." "Ah," Samuel said, "but he isn't really."

"No, he lost his nuts in fair weather. You see? You can't see from there. But you can tell. We were in training together. At first we had cots. Then we got beds with springs. The first day we were sitting around, naked—we did a lot of that. That one jumps up and gets his privates jammed in the springs, pulled them off."

"Why do you have your recruiting office in a church?"

"Consecrated ground. Saintly vocation. You're twenty-two? Haven't done your military service? How's that? Have to do it."

"I am not suited for military service," Samuel replied boldly.

"Eh?"

"I have only one eye."

The sergeant nodded. "Have to. Fifty per cent vision."

"Yes."

"Lost an eye. Does the hole hurt?"

"No," Samuel said; "no." He could smell incense and hear more singing.

"Yes, yes, the army," said the sergeant. "It hurts that one. But not the other one, defender of the faith, the grenade blast." "What do you suppose this paper means?" Samuel asked. It was very cold in the church, damp and dark. The sergeant was waving his claws in time with the music. "Found a home in the army," he said, "haw. All together now, buddies one and all." Then the sergeant explained what Samuel was to do next, and Samuel with a sigh agreed nothing could be simpler. Then the band of penitents and the priest came back and Samuel followed them from the church.

Johnson was a soldier for six years.

Adventure. Privation, windfall, fellowship, daily dread and daily bread. The ups, the downs, sudden death, lingering death, now this and now that, you make the best of it: knifeplay, disembowellings, headplay, decapitations, barracks-cheer, tentfun, pranks and yanks, tears and fears, the kicks, the scared little pricks walking single file in the high scraping grass. Johnson, quite as he had anticipated, had not much skill or interest in war. He was thought a fool and hence escaped being accused of cowardice. Ahead and behind him there was plenty of courage. Wisdom in the field, stealth, night marches, nightmares, bedwettings, dishonorable discharges, but somehow he stuck, he hung on while he observed that an army moves on its belly, rubbing softly back and forth, making strange voluptuous noises, daydreaming in the slime, the primordial slime, the original fault, whence it all arose, whither are we going? he was sometimes asked and he had too much time to try to reply and so only wore the stupid glare of mediocrity, showed the snotface stupidity of a pressed infantryman. Thus he got through at least a dozen campaigns. There, in the heat, in the cold, in the desert and in the swamps, in the iron mountains mouse-grey under the heaven made of white steel and in the choking jungle paris green where old old soldiers it is true never seem to die, young soldiers change color and read scripture. In no matter what unit he served, Johnson's comrades time and time again found God, then lost Him, or were lost in an ambush, or were discovered unfit to continue; for the way to self-knowledge leads past the cliff's edge, oh how swiftly turns the wheel. Learning is acquired, learning is the cause of a thousand indispositions, freshness and grace forsake the body: knowledge hath in it something of the serpent and therefore where it entereth into a man it makes him to swell; scientia inflat... in spacious knowledge there is much contristation. The living rot, its endurance, the soldier's, two years have revolved, then five, a hideous lustrum of soldier hope and soldier joy and soldier bloat. Leaves torn from texts, bloodied and beshitted trucolor illustrations of the Saviour His Passion, paragraphs from the classics and the scholastic thinkers formed a kind of mucus-track denoting their regimental progress; rearguard native troops came after, carefully obliterating the traces. Five years of it and, Johnson found, there was nothing to prevent a boy from turning into an unmanageable man; why! what strength of arms acquired, what woe and pleasure undergone! what is it, for example, to couple with an obedient gun, to quiver behind its infinite concussions, to sense exquisite vibrations in the soul? to set men afire, say? to shoot at them in trees, caves, or from aloft, from high above on high? to wander through battle, one's buttocks trembling, one's sore little pink prick in one's hand, pissing on the faces and feet of the dying? Why, it is adventure, it is experience precious in the schooling of a perfect gentleman; is there any comparable crêche for breeding real killers?

But when all was said and done Johnson decided that although there is much here that appeals to the eye, there was little behind it that flattered his taste; thus, he learned that when it is a question of war, people do speak nonsense; and do they not, my chit? War and speaking, he found, do not go very well together, have you perceived it, eh? And when they're joined, when this nonsense's spoken, this mismatch is in some sort a plea for forgiveness, wouldn't you say? Johnson observed it again and again, so have I—it does me good to talk about Johnson and I shall probably come back to him again; it would have been bleak, bleak had not poor old Marivaux mentioned him this morning—, I have come to suspect there is some inner spring which when touched by the idea of violence, the image of war, releases a hundred consequent outbursts, as when one's sense of the risible stirred, mirth wakes. Oh indeed, a warrior race is a happy chuckling cackling one; and there is something infectious in the way they'll clap their palms to their temples, snatch out handfuls of hair, pop their

eyes at you and say, My God I do not understand or
What madness. It soothes them. At any rate, we
who equally serve all know what are the agonies of
peace, or can imagine them. We all have, somewhere, some sort of mother or wife or sister. Your
letter reminded me of the fact I also soldiered a little.
It was for six years too. However, I had an appointment, I believe. And I was walking through the
bright black streets. I met a few faces. What sad
expressions! what trouble, what sorrow! oh, noble
people, how grief does embellish your features! It
was time, high time to eat.

I reached the rôtisserie—the Maréchal Gilles de
Retz. "The Prince is dead," said Colonel Petterade;
"how are you?" "Thank you," I replied; I remembered your letter and added: "the hour weighs evilly,
icily upon me." "Hot," said General Kuhl, staring,
inert, like his adjutant bolt upright in a wicker chair,
under a parasol, framed by potted shrubberies. "Hot,"
said Petterade, putting on his sun-glasses. "Hup,"
said the general, "war has been declared." "But the
war has never ended," I protested. "No," the general
retorted, "it has been redeclared, reaffirmed." "That
must be done from time to time," said Petterade,
"we find." "Hup," Kuhl repeated. "Waiter," said
Petterade, "tomato juice". "Ice," added Kuhl. "Ice,"
repeated the colonel.

I could, had I wished, left then, for I had found out
what I wanted to know, having come with very little
to ask. A thought occurred to me. "You know,"
I began.

General Kuhl glanced at me for an instant. He
shook his head slowly. "Glory hallelujah," said he
in his quiet, clear-ringing voice. He was born to com-

mand. He had a superb chin, a smooth skin, and looked less than his age. "Sounding forth the trumpets." I smiled; the thought had vanished from my head. "The judgment seat," he said, "the drums."

It was the music of the spheres. This was between men, Aimée. It was a question of the military situation and of military men; the latter did not exactly, in a discursive sense, speak of the former; but what they, those two soldiers did say, what little, what very little they said... Aimée, there are things which are excluded from the understanding, which... but how am I to convey the experience if I am forced to employ a terminology that fails me at every step, every instant? Night has fallen. I am in my room. I imagine we are entered into a tenebrous realm and are having to do with brute entities, existential and self-contained, free beings, that is to say, amongst which obtain affirmative relations only. I ask whether there is communion between those celestial bodies whereupon our wondering gaze is drawn; is there a commerce, a correspondence between those inert, immutable, purely existing objects? Ah, I believe so.

Petterade ordered the waiter to fetch lemon-peel for the tomato juice, lemon-peel, salt, pepper, nutmeg.

I imagine a dialogue; I imagine one substantive effusing its intelligence of objective being, and saying —by means of I know not what organ, through unresonant space—to the other, its twin: "Thou art there, I am here." Whereunto answer is made by its double: " I am here, be thou there." "I shalt be here eternally provided thou rest and thou wilt rest forever in my resting."—What did the colonel and the general say? They manifested their existence, their existing presence, they confronted me and one

another, looking serenely upon themselves, and so,
limpidly, they transmitted the military situation,
re-creating it, exhaling it, their morphological selves
were its dramatization and a commentary upon it.
Aimée, do I hear you object? Go softly there; say,
if you like, that you do not understand, I expected
you would not, I should say no more about the matter
were I not certain you would protest against my silence.
Is it the silence you hate, oh unquiet woman? But,
what's this? Does not every woman admire the fine
young soldier, his neat tonsure, his erect carriage,
his simple, honest heart, regular features, gay costume,
his deeds, the things he has done, the places he has
been? Who more lovable, more loving than the
soldier? his firm flesh, his little tongue. It has been
remarked, astutely, I believe, that it is almost always
difficult and even more often dolorous for military
men to speak of anything—I have known cases in
which a trooper would flay or be flayed, tear out a
captive's fingernails or, a captive, have them one by
one snatched from his fingers, beat or be beaten into
a jelly by bamboo rods, prefer to give or be put to
any torture rather than unseal his lips, pronounce
a syllable; this is fixity, courage, honor, the devotion
and will which all alone make our world what it is,
make it go—and the more military the man, the less
the magnificent fellow is articulate. "But these officers
of yours were ordinary men, were they not?" "Ordinary? Prototypal specimens." "Primitive?" "Primitive, I should say so, and pure." "And I take it you
would maintain purity, in the conventional sense,
is mute?" I would. Mute save when it is a question
of purity; and then purely eloquent: the eloquence
of the pure soldier announces the military situation,

nothing else: confronted by the pure soldier, you are in the presence of the military situation in all its purity, in all its pure overwhelming intensity; we are evidently dealing here with what passes for the soldierly temper; it is, we too often forget, the effect of the soldierly constitution, of, that is to say, the vital parts, the privities, which, in a warrior of the purest lineage, in a thoroughbred, a prize-winner, are commonly peculiarly developed or undeveloped; these pretended defects (which are virtues, tokens of virtue, and shortcomings only in terms of that vicious civilization whose terminology, I repeat, I have no choice but to adopt) are compensated for by the attributes and faculties which designate the strong silent from the incontinent, garrulous, frivolous and promiscuous type. Has anything been more frequently or more conclusively demonstrated? the man of action has only to be plunged into civil surroundings, into this welter of persiflage, this whirlpool of impudicities and he at once becomes subject to the most imperious urges, racked by the most unbearable tensions; everything he sees about him affronts his delicacy, he is revolted by all, shocked by this material nightmare, his very soul is assailed, exacerbated. Everything rubs, tickles, itches, bites, excites, arouses him. He is soon inflamed, maddened; he will run amok, he will disport, break, trample, wreck. What else can he do? Be sure of it, he will do his best; his best will do all the doing. How is he to signal his depthless abhorrence of all these *conditions?* Or rather, how else if not by shattering what menaces him? Incapable of imitating the suave gibbering of the polite, he is forced to resort to violence—what? it is no resort, no substitute at all, and he acts with a glad heart. Civil law, unnatural law, blasphemous law proscribes violence: what a temptation to flaunt and demolish those injunctions! The soldier finds himself in an impasse whence he cannot escape without sacrificing some of his purity which, once gone, makes him to grieve ever after. Attempting to extricate himself from the damning compromise imposed by civilization, the soldier is driven now and again to irregularities, to give vent to declamatory outbursts, abusive gestures, acts whose purpose is, precisely, to affirm the very kind of pure existence maculative language tends perpetually to deny. Tormented, I repeat, tormented by this confusion cherished and nurtured by the non-spiritual civilized spirit, the true, the pure, the essential soldier is periodically taken by what resemble hysteric and tuneful seizures; the singing to which military men are especially addicted is invariably misprized by the cultivated... Yes, Aimée, you behold it now; this digression was then for the better. And now back to Colonel Petterade and General Kuhl.

The waiter has brought a tasty, thin soup; we all three blow upon our spoons to cool the liquid, then we swallow a little, next we blow, then swallow, blow again, and yet another swallow. Unhappily, I am unable to report their conversation in detail or render its nuances or quality: strictly viewed, it contained nothing like details, nor nuances, and only a fugitive quality; strictly viewed, it was not a conversation at all, nor talk, nor speech, no, none of that, my dear, not in the conventional sense, but a steady and fascinating sound, like that made by smooth objects of great weight and bulk moving at very great speed through space so vast as to baffle most ordinary perceptions of motion, confuse all estimates of weight

and size: it might be conceived of as a chanted invocation, to shift our approach somewhat, a whistling,
an ethereal suspiration which, I assure you, is not to
be reproduced in cold blood. You observe the problems I have to tackle. They've done up thirty historians in the past five years. My personal business
is to be familiar with the military situation, it has a
capital influence upon what I am chronicling; we are
a warrior Nation from top to bottom, through and
through. I used perhaps once a fortnight, or even
three times a month, indeed as often as was necessary,
I used, I say, to lend a trained ear to the extraordinary vibrations a little patience, oh, a little wheedling,
a little coquetry may yet induce generals and colonels
to emit. These sessions have become rarer. Actually,
they are always the same. One covers the same ground.
Naturally enough, one gets a little fed up.

A stew à la bourbonnaise, the Maréchal Gilles'
spécialité militaire, was served us next.

That stew doesn't vary much either.

The military situation, of which I had, I tell you,
a wealth of prior knowledge gathered during innumerable get-togethers of, it bears repeating, this same
sort, and whose by and large unchanged state the
pure expression of these officers allowed me to infer,
was (has always been, apparently) and is as follows :
what has been sometimes called—

But here a cautionary note: these are crude approx-
imations: the impure act of description imparts its
impurity to the pure situation described. What, to
our perpetual shame, has been with shocking looseness
called a limited police action, an exercize (Operation
Prepuce) at battalion strength, an operation (Perfo-
rate) embracing a restricted area but of some pro-

fundity, against fractionists, separatists and bandits, a display of faith, firmness and uncompromising devotion to ideal and tradition, over a somewhat broader area and against veteran opponents, a religious crusade, being a battle for men's minds and sacred ends, a spirited defense of the obol, a disinterested attempt to check aggression and protect related powers, a war of liberation, a last-ditch stand to save Grön from a handful of thieves and tax-evaders, common malefactors of the petty kind, small bands of fanatics, plainly organized and probably in foreign pay, certain unscrupulous tribal leaders acting upon low motives and perversely, whole villages of opium-smokers and priest-murderers, also frenzied and depraved, blackamoor rebels, bloodthirsty, unprincipled, devil-worshipping, armed with better than spears, with pamphlets and worse, false-coiners, obol-wreckers, insidious and deft saboteurs, risen provinces, tumultuous populations of enslaving slaves, mutually subordinating, reciprocally tyrannical, and by the subtlest imaginable devices autodespotical, a ruthless, sworn enemy, mightily ambitious, irredentistic, panblackamoorian, whose victory would precipitate the *finis Latinorum*, is still in progress.

"Never call retreat. The hearts of men," said Kuhl, tossing down a glass of milk, "be swift."

Yes, these various operations, successively mounted against these several opponents, have been conducted in jungles, forests, swamps, deserts, hills, plains, hamlets, towns, cities, upon rivers, bays, estuaries, the open sea, in a word, they have fought wherever possible, in the open air and in human consciences and in the hearts of men at night and during the day, summer, autumn, winter and spring, without interruption;

the contending forces, now large, now small, have struggled more or less at random, according to no immediately available scheme, for no definite objectives, and often for no apparent reason, now vigorously, valorously and with resounding success, now sluggishly and with none whatever, occasionally this war of movement has been moved with exceptional audacity and bravoure, both completely fruitless, and then, slipping into another declension, with singular lassitude and faintheartedness which have yielded threefold and four, make of that what you will, and our national novelists, all seven hundred of them, and our two poets have incessantly treated this war, not very successfully, I'd judge. The theatre of conflict has been located in the East, located there, that is to say, by common opinion which, although not invariable, might, I dare say, be consulted today and found to incline orientally, whether for logically sound reasons or for the not entirely unsound reason that, in ages past, much mischief has been wrought against Grön by easterly powers; in the absence of explicit information, none being supplied by our automatic writers, the popular imagination falls back upon penchant and folklore; the which, seasoned with noble old prejudices, may provide, as has proven true in this instance, inspiration quite as valid as what may be had from any other source.

"Drink deep," said Petterade, touching my shoulder.

For all indications seem to concur and jointly to propose that the agitated area has shifted, dwindled, enlarged, and does those things yet, owing to a multitude of factors equally unstable and hard to ascertain. The last thirty-one years of reprisal, retorsion, retaliation, re-establishment of order, resistance to satan-

ical empiry, and desperate self-defense has cost Grön
216 billion obols; or an average of about OB 7/year (1).
After God knows how many years of fighting, casualties
in this just, necessary, unwanted, infamous, inevitable,
ruinous, savage, suicidal and glorious war have reached, according to very reputable inferences, the startling
figure of 2,967,086, usually arrived at thus:

TABLE I

	Killed	Wounded	Missing	Prisoners
Army	287,830	2,522,404	0	?
Navy	11,786	3,009	0	?
Air Force	66,256	75,590	211	?
Total	365,872	2,601,003	211	?

and sometimes, by those whose arguments merit close
attention also and who otherwise perceive the thing,
thus:

TABLE II

	Killed	Wounded	Missing	Prisoners
Army	?	0	2,522,404	287,830
Navy	?	0	3,009	11,786
Air Force	?	211	75,590	66,256
Total	?	211	2,601,003	365,872

(1) 1 obol = 7 shillings 4½d.

Bizarre arithmetic, I own. Consider for a moment that our population has never at any given time exceeded twelve million persons. 2,967,086 is an estimate. A strange one, nevertheless. Why, yes! for this is a strange war, my pet. Also, we have allies. Certainly, we must have allies; how else is one to account for the 2,967,086? And I dare say they have suffered frightfully, those poor bleeders. I find it difficult to concentrate at the moment. Well, refer now to the tables. Notice that while they both agree upon the gross total of losses, which would come to 2,967,086, they are at variance when they assign a nature and hence a specific cause to them, thereby pronouncing discongruous opinions upon what is of the essence; yet, the differences appear to be eliminated, mark you, the breach seems to close again when either table, discovering a shared and symmetrical doubt, distills, through interrogatory signs and zeros, the very same hesitancy, excess of caution, or perturbation. Nevertheless, lo! cleavage recurs when it becomes plain that the insufficiency of each table admits of various interpretations simultaneously of the spirit of the tabulator and the spirit of the war, how it is being conducted, etc. What, in fine, has been the fate of the participants? uncertain, that much is clear. What has been the fate of the non-participants (supposing, for a moment and for the sake of discussion, that there is such a thing as non-participation)? they would seem to fall into two categories: those who are partisan to Table I; those who are partisan to Table II. Severally regarded, these partisans are either persons who believe in the justice, necessity, unwantedness, infamy, inevitability, ruin, savagery, suicidal character and glory of this war, ascribe their belief to those pure persons waging it,

71

or partake of that belief and consequently of the purity
after having ascribed both, assimilate themselves into
participants, and positively, constructively behold the
matter, well, properly, admirably; or are persons who
disbelieve in the justice, necessity, unwantedness, etc.,
of this war, ascribe their unbelief to and consequently besmirch, bewray, and degrade those persons
waging it, or sympathize with that unbelief, degra-
dation, and foulness they imagine pre-existent, either
feign a total and very culpable indifference to the war
or assimilate themselves into participants but, by tip-
ping the scales against death and mutilation and in
favor of truancy, pusillanimity, poltroonery, etc., nega-
tively, treasonably behold the matter; and there is a
world of difference. And like that of the participants,
the fate of the non-participants (non-existent though
they turn out to be) is dual: sweet and bitter. Thus,
there are two possible fates for all concerned, and all
are concerned, and those fates are a world apart.
Properly speaking (however impossible it is to speak
properly of the military situation) there is no neutrality
here, no median attitude.   And that is one of the
two great conclusions to be drawn from this figuration
of the military situation which *qua* situation is unfigur-
able, discarnate, ineffable, a holy mystery, very deep,
very distant, a presence from afar, at one and the same
time here upon us and also twenty thousand kilometers
away. The other conclusion is that this presence is
contemporarily all but ubiquitous, the military situation has progressed to the point at which, save for
a few rare exceptions, it has conquered the popular
conscience, absorbed it, and set its stamp upon the
flesh of our sort, our race; the triumph of the revolution to which the Accuser swore his dedication is

within sight; the monster is well nigh slain. It is its death-throes I have the task to record, apparently. Well, that's not as easy as it might seem.

Perhaps it would have been better to save most of this for the end. But, then again, it's not far off.

However, "No mercy, no quarter, jubilation," as Kuhl put it at twenty minutes of two this afternoon.

Four soldiers jog past, halt, shoot, continue on their way.

I bid my acquaintances farewell and struggle off into the heat, the spécialité militaire swishing about in my belly.

Part the Second:

LOVE

Sixty-four years old at the time of the coup d'état, seventy-seven at his death, Pricker John Stearnes of Wim, the most celebrated of his age's finders, was one of those persons who appear to metaphysicians as epiphenomena and, like the discovery of the wheel or gunpowder, as primary material to historians. Stearnes, documents attest, dwelt in no close harmony with his times; he held them at his mercy and contributed heavily to giving their temper and direction to our own. It is not here a question of richness of intellect, breadth of conscience, depth of sensibility, nor of charm, nor wit, but only of a brilliant career: this prodigiously active, low-born patriot, this irresistible visionary, this impassioned reformer, this very dangerous man performed not great deeds but a multitude of small ones, petty and ruinous public services: he amputated many an attainted limb from the body social; his contribution has been recognized in a hundred memorials; but—rare thing—the government has manifested singular caution in his regard, and his influence—as in the case of the influence of certain parasitical creepers, bloodsucking worms, and policemen—has never been officially qualified as in the main beneficial or harmful.

At least eight thousand Grönards, tears in their eyes, hearts beating with emotion, participated at the enigmatic Pricker's obsequies in the Carrefour des Martyrs. The second air marshal, Fundament-Pfut, presided; his harangue, "John Stearnes: butcher or surgeon?" crowded with guarded statements and

77

counter-proposals, was long. "Appearances are likely to deceive—" "Yes, yes," his auditors chirped, like St Francis' sparrows. "—and let them," Fundament-Pfut concluded. "Aye." "Demolish the illusion, and straightway all the world regrets it. Therefore," the pilot pursued, "let us be charitable, especially since the object of our tolerant philosophy is Stearnes, in whose connection, that he be understood aright, my friends, there is copious charity, tolerance and philosophy needed. Hastily scanned, his record sits in the shadow; the light of your love will whiten it. Seemingly, he deserves your hatred—oh sacred simplicity! it is not to be denied: John Stearnes was a cruel man.

"But pause," Fundament-Pfut cried, putting down his text; "stay; some of you have come to send our good John off with a curse: will those of you who believe him bad increase his stature? would you thus rashly, tragically dishonor your kin his hand honored? Evil John? Ah, I call out for justice," said Fundament-Pfut, picking up his papers again, "for reason, friends, for tact and common sense. Make the effort; it is becoming; it is prudent; it is easy; see if it is not agreeable to forgive; see whether there is anything a cruel man may not be forgiven—" "Hear, hear!" piped up a university student. "—and ponder upon the necessity for cruelty, if what is bitter in life is to be sweetened at all." These words were thunderously applauded. "He engineered, did our gentle John, the ruin of your father? His tongue or pins brought about your brother's death? Then their blood is on Stearnes' hands: you knew him well: say, did he not bear his cross christianly? No man will contradict me; what one will not join me when I say Stearnes is more to be commiserated than withered by an utterly vain spite? Say it once with me: he kept the Devil from me. 'Twas very well done of him, was it not? Pray for John. Love our eminent, most lamented Pricker. Ladies—" At this point a cannon boomed; they sniffled and dabbed their eyes, and John Stearnes was inhumated reverently and with display.

Before he became great and good and beloved, unreflective common opinion, prone to misjudging the truly sincere, used once to consider Stearnes a crazy, ridiculous fellow, a nuisance, a prattler, meriting no trust and unclean. He lacked friends, was without family; he skulked about by night and hid in his hut by day. He was, in truth, poor and often hungry. He'd filch a cabbage or a carrot from a garden and would have been forgiven, indeed helped or fed, had it not been for his vulgar coarse tongue and grey awful eye; he was a fright to see: wens and carnosities grew all over his face, his mood was such they fancied there must be boils on his body, a pallid-skinned, scabby, frail body he kept wrapped up in ragged black woollens, winter and summer.

There one day came to Wim a poor wretch, a pedlar, who, trembling and stammering, told them at the tavern that while passing through the forest he had been accosted by a malign spirit; for what else, he asked, could it have been? Had he not been a stout and able man, goodly sized and strong? It was a great black dog that came up to him, with fearful fiery eyes, long teeth and a terrible countenance and, said the pedlar, the beast had looked him in the face. And now by the Devil's art his head was drawn awry, his eyes and face deformed, his speech not well to be understood, his thighs and legs stark lame, his arms lame, especially the left arm; his hands cramped and turned out of their course; his body scarce able to endure travel: such was he now, in this plight; naught he cared to sell his wares and, once he had told his story, he dragged himself off and was gone. "Lord," said Roger Gascoing, "a great black dog froze him in the wood."

And then there comes a hailstorm in mid-July, and it's followed by a flood. Some fields are blasted, the crops die, the land is salted, it seems, and Mrs. Gudge's girl Susie has fits and vomits ten-penny nails. "Might be the régime's being changed, or they're planning," suggests Benjamin Boot. A granary burns. "Seems sure they'll raise the taxes," William Winesap comments. "Makes your throat dry," says Roger and they have more ale in silence. They might, who knows, have come to fancy it was Stearnes' doing; but the old man's quicker than they and immediately starts his denunciations and civic gestures. He goes to the tavern—they'd never seen him set foot there before—and declares he's been five times wounded defending his country, believes in God Almighty and such-and-such an one does not. Benjamin spits at Stearnes, William's about to strike him when he brings it tumbling out that Elisabet Vlamyncx has two enchanted toads, they're named Jeso and Carabin, Jimmy Og keeps a brace of taught ferrets, Colinette Gascoing a very maleficient rat that waits on her and which she calls Pyewacket and suckles at a teat under her armpit. Colinette's husband Roger, a big man, is there; "Roger," Boot asks, "is all that true?" Stifling with rage and confusion, Roger utters not a word. "I say, Roger."

"Eh?"

"Speak up, Roger," cries Winesap, "what about it? John here maintains—"

"No, by God!" Roger shouts, very red in the face, squeezing his hands into fists, "no, it's not true, I don't think it's true," but Roger's got a puzzled look now. Outside, the wind stirs in the dry leaves. The innkeeper goes to shut the door, to slip the bolt.

"Aren't you sure, Roger?"

Stearnes blows his nose.

"What about it, Roger?"

"Where was Colinette last Saturday night?" Stearnes asks him.

"Last Saturday night?" The big man's hands open and close, his chest rises and falls.

"Was she in your bed?"

"No," says Roger in a little voice, "she was at her sister's place, helping Gellie."

"Helping her do what, Roger?"

Stearnes laughs like a knife scraping a tin dish. "The two of them weren't off on a ride, were they? She wouldn't have been helping sister Gellie kiss the fiend's asshole?"

"Do you think it's witches, John?" the others ask, and he replies:

"With these two eyes I saw Elisabet Vlamyncx go out into Peter Whicklethorp's field—Joseph Johnson was with her—it was about midnight—and while the Devil held the plough, Elisabet yoked her toads to it, and then Joseph Johnson drove it; the harness was couch-grass, the trace-chains too, a gelded animal's horn was the coulter, and a piece of the same was the sock; and when they'd done ploughing and damning Peter Whicklethorp's field, Joseph lets out a shout: 'Maikpeblis!' he yells and the demon vanishes, so do

81

the plough and the toads, and Joseph and Elisabet go off together right pleased with themselves."

Catherine Volmar, he affirmed, was wedded to Devil Peterlin and could cure a bloated cow and make it talk and often did. They all, he swore, had lewd and unlawful commerce with the Fiend, were marked by him; that he could prove. "You can prove it, John?" "Aye," says he. Wherewith up they got and went to Judge Guillaumin's house; Stearnes recites all his stories through again; Colinette's fetched in, Roger's swearing at her, he gives her a cuff, her face is gone white, there are circles under her eyes. "Well," says the Judge. And the hero begins his pricking and mumbling straight off and for nearly two hours Roger holds his woman upright, sometimes weeping, sometimes execrating her, now calling Colinette his darling and his life and hugging her to him, now roaring abominable things and clutching her tighter yet, while Stearnes runs his long pin into Colinette's naked flesh, till at last he thrusts it all along its way into her heart, covers the swallowed steel with his thumb, and says, with a mournful expression on his perspiring old face:

"Look ye there."

He removes his thumb; no blood's come from the wound. "That's it," mutters Stearnes, "the Devil's place." They were amazed and Colinette's corpse was burned, Roger too. A storm howled that night, the wind fanned the blaze and scattered all the ashes.

Stearnes directed them to swim Elisabet, Catherine confessed on the rack, spitting Boots and the skeptical Winesap defended themselves very badly. Stearnes called himself God's Witch-Pricker Indicated; thereafter he had his way with the humble and the mighty.

They sold Jimmy Og's lands and chattels when he was burned and with what proceeded purchased seven silver pins; these an abbot blessed and these the parish of Wim solemnly entrusted to Stearnes. That then was the transitional period, such was life in the country during the waning hours of the Republic, this was the disorder science and a more centralized government were to repair, not by rudely jolting popular traditions, but by inclining, rectifying them almost imperceptibly, by adapting them to the circumstances modern life imposes. It used to be that poor, aged, ill-favored dames, spinsters and widows, young women too, and girls, lads and infants and lonely old men alike were regularly burned or strangled or drowned the second Friday of every month, often thirteen at a stroke; it used to be the common prayer in middle age in one breath confusedly to ask deliverance for oneself and to ask that Stearnes be delivered, to groan to be spared and to entreat God, or one's Master, that one be taken off quick and early and not to be made to last for the boots, the pilliewinkis and the stake. These crudities, these Gothicisms are today gone by; it is not now bones we crush, nor open-air bonfires we light, nor by identical methods we interrogate culprits, nor similar hints of depravation we look for. When Claude-Maxime became Grön's prince and all the bustle and to-do of delations and enquiries entered a completely new phase, the State had need of capable hands, experts deep-learned and astute, steadfast officers and juries. Scouts ranged far into the provinces to enlist what talent there was there; Stearnes' immense reputation assured him an interview, his comportment before the Accuser's lieutenants gained him their recommendation, ten days had scarcely elapsed before he had pricked one of them and arranged the swimming of the other; established in Grön, the whimsical old moralist instigated such a quantity of combustions he won himself a favorite's place, a fortune, and life tenure.

At Lammastide in the twelfth year John Stearnes had out his maps and schedules, his almanacks and all his scrying tackle. "O Bloodybones!" he muttered, his glance sticking at some abominable conjunction of suasions and ascendancies, meaningless to the untried, perhaps, but freighted, bursting with significance for John. Rapidly, breathing hoarsely, scenting crime and evil congruence, he checked his numbers; they stood. He grabbled in his pocket; withdrew a morocco grain case stamped with the curious seal of the Witch-Prickers Guild. From an assortment of pretty five-inch pins he selected a clean point, passed it through an alcohol flame, wrapped it in sterilized cotton, slipped pin and wrapping into an aluminum tube, poured ten or twelve drops of alcohol into the tube, poured ten or twelve drops of Calvados into a glass, screwed a brass cap onto the tube, drained the glass, put the tube into a pocket and the empty glass on a shelf; made one last frantic review of his calculations and inspired juxtapositions; no, nothing was amiss there. Papers flew, his pencil marked, his head was scratched, his nose picked, his anus tickled and poked, for Stearnes had not enjoyed security as a child; he lifted the telephone—the wire led straight to the Minister of the Interieur's apartments.

"What an agreeable surprise; how pleasant to hear your voice, John," grunted Grimoald. "What's on for today?" Stearnes related the tale told by the stars God's own finger moves, the reliable stars, the unfailing finger, and made his divulgences; they were as usual most welcome, but "I'm afraid I haven't got a regiment of the guard to spare. After Thursday —you couldn't put it off until next week?" Hardly. Stearnes' voice was acid. Grimoald hedged. Stearnes resorted to irony.

"Henry," he began.

"John."

"Henry, do you suppose the Devil will relent—"

"No, John."

"—or retard his black conspiratorial activities or suspend his unspeakably malevolent intentions to suit your convenience? Do you suppose he will imitate rather than profit from your hesitations? Oh, sweet innocence! no. He has ever been in motion since his expulsion from the skies, is now and always shall be taking his bitter revenge upon order, upon culture, upon—"

"I'll find a company—"

"Even a battalion of superior beserks... oh, Henry, I dread the issue. There is a mighty confidence grounded upon nothing, which swaggers and huffs and swears there are no witches; among the better bred and looser gentry there are those that dare not bluntly to say there is no God: they are content to deny spirits. Atheism is begun in sadducism."

"A good company. All virgins, John."

"All virgins?"

"How many revolutionaries have you got there?"

"I count thirteen covens, one hundred and sixty-nine individual rebels, anarchists, retrograde socialists and creeping collectivists in all, very desperate men, very vindictive, many of them skilled in military arts, and all profoundly bad."

"I'll have the boys there at four."

"No later."

"Good night, John."

"Ware thee well, Henry."

Stearnes clapped on his pointed black hat and invisible cloak and rushed out to complete his preparations. When everything was readied he went in the direction of St Bridget's Fields, by the prisons and the factories, a melancholy place, where he planned to hide himself that caressing greatmooned night, and wait.

* *

The two blades of a horizontal fan swam through the muggy air, whose eddies lifted moths and little flies drugged by the heavy atmosphere; these insects floated upwards to click and bounce against a spotty yellowish ceiling and to fumble about neon fixtures that cast an ice-cream parlor light, sticky and pink; then these insects, as a rule, would fall to the glass top of the desk over which crouched Henry Grimoald, drowsy, in his shirtsleeves, smoking a cigarette and thinking of his duty, which he loved to perform but not to think about. He was thinking of the obstacles between him and the performance of what he was there, in that room, nine hours a day, so much doing was there to be done, to do. Now, the idea of performance introduced one of theatre, of acting, and for Grimoald acting, once named, once recognized and nakedly designated, was sham; his thoughts hitched back to the obstacles that were preventing him from doing the thing properly and making him think about it instead: this room, for example, and he emitted an oath, then a sigh: it was insolid, it didn't convince him, never had, he was no fool, it was like a stage set, stage paint, putty and plaster, a room in a building made of concrete mixed six or eight parts sand to one of cement. The building, and one would never believe it, was only four years old; to be sure, rainfall during those particular four years had been a fraction in excess of normal.

So many things tend to melt away. A state is so vulnerable, so frail, it spoils so easily. Grimoald put a peppermint in his mouth. And men, he thought, take men for example, there are so few you can count upon to do a good job, for the job is often as not a pretty bad one that needs doing, and the sort that usually does it best is, sadly enough, a son of a bitch whom you wouldn't trust to escort your aging mother to the neighborhood euthanasia station; no, it's worry, worry, worry.

The Objector forced his way into the Minister's office. It was even more difficult to shut than to open the door which was warped as well as improperly hung. The Objector pushed, kicked, wood scraped on wood, several flakes of paint, some more moths and little flies drifted down, and the neon winked.

"Easy there, fracas, fracas," said Grimoald, peering at a paperclip he had wedged under a fingernail. "You've got it straight, haven't you? It's St Bridget's Fields, at four, tonight, and then tomorrow, or the next day, a speedy trial or something like that." The Objector opened his mouth. "No," Grimoald cautioned, "none of that, don't talk, don't ask questions, don't say anything to me. Hold yourself in, save your strength for the sprint, then show your class, but not here, I'm tired."

"It's warm weather."

Grimoald squinted at the man in evening dress, clean-shaven, episcopal; he shook his head, wondering what the future would bring, and looked through the open window at the darkness that soothed his aching eyes. "How's Claude-Maxime's heart?" he demanded, uselessly, and at the same instant feeling it was not really a question he was putting to this man, but this man's answer to it he was analyzing. For, most impenetrable of a host of contemporary enigmas, most hard to believe of all absurdities, this curiosity facing him, this compound of marshmallow and sound, had, according to persistent rumor, that is to say according to the highest authority, been chosen the Prince's successor.

Advancing rapidly, Grimoald had moved almost out of range of the words, "This heat represents a peril for those subject to cardiac affections"; the Objector, Grimoald could hardly avoid noticing, had pale blue eyes behind his rimless octagonal glasses... thinning straight dark brown hair, a ruddy complexion, a wide thin-lipped mouth that suggested a readiness to whine, an infantile mouth filled with small even teeth, heavy build, height five feet ten inches, weight about two hundred and ten pounds, no distinguishing characteristics, no visible scars; "doctors tell me." A small flash of rage pricked the Minister of the Interior. He flung away the paper clip and began licking a red spot near that place where the nail reaches over the sensitive flesh at the finger's tip.

* * *

For above a week there had been disturbances at the railway station and around it in one of the oldest quarters of Grön. The troubles began afresh every morning, lasted late and even kept up round the clock.

Several causes were at work here: foremost among them was a recrudescence of popular indocility: of what, in turn, there were certain who wondered, of what, in turn, was a recrudescence of popular indocility the effect? Disease, ignorance, error, idleness. Suspicions had been activated by seditious voices, by malcontents, by mad-dog train-wreckers and spies and every species of cabalist and calumniator and rabid humanist, among them persons of wealth and family, education and good breeding.

The state was also discomfited by another virtually complete economic paralysis and its accompaniments, wholesale unemployment and deflation; here were a few more clues. A handful of unstable spirits and hotheads had mutinied in a propellor factory. Some impudent fellows had pelted a tank with stones and then each other with excrements. A band of women had presented themselves at the Ministry of Public Works, delivered a petition, and distributed obscene toys to the civil employees. Alarmed by their example and, fortunately, misinterpreting it, many others, confused by hunger, had clumsily expressed their love for the Accuser and implacable confidence in his leadership by acquitting themselves of tumultuous acts of faith—no, don't think for a minute there is any short-cut method of sounding the people's motives; your arithmetical polltakers and piebrained statisticians shabbily conceal their contempt for men when, enviously, it sometimes seems to me, they describe them as marionettes moved by threads. Your economical strings, I assure you, and your naturalists' ropes contain very Gordian knots, and for every puppet you watch manipulated with success you hang twenty-six others. At any rate, my dear, the people ran to riot and massacred a sizable fraction of the first of three army battalions that arrived from the coast. These were handpicked, inferior troops; their disastrous overseas record was exemplary; this was the culminating hour of their nicely-calculated expenditure.

Customary procedure required that, in collaboration with the Bureau of Indication, a Committee of Four—Grimoald and three adjutants: Colonel Bougre of Psychological Warfare, Judge Porn of the Ministry of Justice and Beaux Arts, Father Shart of the Ministry of Information—prepare the homecoming ceremony; "Defense of our Homes" was the pivot upon which everything was made to turn. The citizens were alerted. Their secret forebodings were confirmed by a team of publicists directed by Shart. What might be the soldiers' mood in defeat? what of these diseases they could be and according to much received reports indeed were bringing back with them? Bougre proposed the idea of an epidemic as a prelude to the subtler infections by which Porn set such store. The Committee voted an ambiguous repression. The ceremony's second phase imposed itself mechanically: the most inflammatory bruit was sped through the city: after a prolonged exposure to a climate of depravation crowned by the oriental rout, there had been a thoroughgoing corruption accomplished in the boys, for the greater part inexperienced and susceptible, and to escape at all, they being cruelly reduced, they had pledged their very souls; there would surely be looting and worse, for the young men had slipped off every ethical restraint; the soldiers' skin had turned yellow, or brown, or black, their hair black and straight or frizzy black, the wave and gloss were gone, dear God the honey-hued flesh tint too; their cheekbones had risen prominently, their noses had flattened, got wide, their lips puffed, that was how they'd look; there had occurred a horrid alteration in their tastes; they'd best be dealt with as prudence bids one treat with a crazed beast; they knew how to dissemble their new natures and were not to be trusted, regardless of their professions or feints, they were artful; the distemper would be manifest later, the infection burned slow; therefore strike early, with a heavy heart and determined arm; that was the safer and more sympathetic way to take with them, for they were suffering innerly; spare your children; these wolves, these monsters had an appetite for young flesh; and the Asiatic preference for tender behinds, an intellectual air, were full of quotations, pacific attitudes that deceive, would cross their arms while filthy designs bred in their hearts. The order went out to unweapon the returning troops and simultaneously to permit a few firearms and a meagre store of ammunition to fall into the hands of the mob. In every quarter, continually, discreet prodding; the élite guard was to be employed now here, now there, sometimes a blow aimed against the crowd, sometimes one against the converts, all that indifferently but deftly and with a maximum of noise, smoke and trampling.

This was the masterfully orchestrated tolly-polly that awaited, among others, young Johnson's company, or, more precisely, its remnants, for there were many missing out of the ranks and what criminals were left in them were to varying degrees invalided by fever, cuts, bruises, burns, blasts and punctures. To varying degrees, be it noted; however sorry, that was nevertheless an eminently dangerous and cut-throat crew that pulled in on time, at seven on the dot. They were all conscriptees: all had been impressed into, not one had offered himself voluntarily for the service of the State every sensible little shaver, it goes quite without saying, ought to be all afire to defend; and this fact of their common delinquency, their backhanging, uninspiration and morose cynicism speaks whole libraries of their character and, were the least justification for it ever to be sought, would excuse whatever the measure an enlightened government might take, might, urged on by popular outcry, reluctantly be forced to take to prevent their contamination of society.

Those bandits, not one of whom was out of his twenties, were amazed and grimly confided one to the other they had never seen and surely never expected anything quite like the commotion that swirled through the station; they wondered what to do. Although suffering from a scalp-wound and his head done up in bandages, Johnson, who stood apart from his copains, for he had been given a disciplined upbringing and a quantity of instruction very appropriate to situations like the present one, and in whom there had been inculcated modesty, reserve and much political science, kept his head clutched in his hands and proposed to the others that, since the goings-on outside eclipsed anything they had encountered in war and since they had only been trained to go to it and their counsellors had neglected mention of how to behave upon one's return, it would perhaps be best for them to remain patiently where they were, like sheep or sitting ducks, and await further developments.

"That's right," cried an officer who had boarded the train that same instant; he advanced in leaps and bounds, brandishing two revolvers and using hard language. "Who's in charge here?" There was no reply. "You," he said, "are you a non-commissioned officer?"

"No, sir," said Johnson.

"What's the f'ck'n' trouble? They all dead?"

"Yes, sir," Johnson murmured.

"Stiff," the officer commented. He introduced himself as Captain Petitcon. "You might call this a f'ck'n' battlefield," said that pure military man, "mightn't you? I think I'd better commission you on it—but don't forget it's tentative and subject to review and approval. What's your name?"

"Samuel Johnson, Captain Petitcon."

"Lieutenant Johnson from now on," said Petitcon, flinging back a lock of clean taffy-colored hair; "Ha! What do you think of that? Stiff," and Captain Petitcon fired through the plateglass window; fired from the hip. "Stiff," he repeated. He was a crack shot. "Well, Sam, what's your f'ck'n' outfit? Company B, Regiment C, Division D? E Army? Well, I say that's f'ck'n' stiff, too bad, I mean for you, f'ck'n' bad luck, very stiff. And this," said he, gesturing with a gun, "this is all there is left? Not much, not very f'ck'n' much. Well, Sam, we'll just sit tight a while. They'll find some others. Get 'em to start singing."

"Singing, Captain Petitcon?"

"Spiritual songs, the blues, all that. Keep it low, they'd better hum, let's have some sad stuff for home-coming. Where'd you say you had the weapons? Eh? Can't make out what you're saying through those f'ck'n' bandages."

"I said, Captain—can you hear me now?"

"Go ahead," said Petitcon, "that's fine."

"I said that we lost all our weapons in the latest of our unsuccessful engagements."

"Lost them all? You mean they took every f'ck'n' pistol and every f'ck'n' rifle and every f'ck'n' thing away from you? Who did it? The f'ck'n' natives, eh? Well, my ass. No? F'ck'n' hard to hear you," the Captain complained. "Don't let them stop singing. Let's have *Mother's Goiter* or *I yearn for Grön.* Which f'ck'n' natives are you talking about?"

"The inhabitants of St Luc."

"St Luc? When you landed?"

"Directly we landed one week ago."

"What've you been doing for a whole f'ck'n' week?"

"Following our reverse we took our ease on the beach, having been denied entrance to the town," Johnson shouted above his comrades' uproar.

"That's stiff," Petitcon shouted back, slipping cartridges into one revolver. "What's that? Some of the men are thirsty? Morphine? Sam, you're right, that's not the blues. Tell them they've got to stop that f'ck'n' moaning and act like heroes, tell them, you've got authority now. Hey, Sam, send a detail to the end of the coach. There's a lot of stuff piled up there near the door; I want it all brought right in here." Four men were appointed to fetch the gear to which Petitcon alluded. Brass gongs and cymbals, small tom-toms, large wooden drums covered with curious painted decorations, masks, feathers, rattles made of calabashes, pipes, flutes, little bells, drumsticks fashioned out of thighbones, animal skins were distributed amongst forty degraded soldiers. "A little music, Sam," Petitcon ordered, "all together now, one, two, three, start playing those things, a little f'ck'n' music."

"How agreeably we get on," Johnson sighed. "That's right," answered Petitcon, darting from window to window, taking cover, popping up, firing, "you're my sort of man."

> *Oh how I burn*
> *It's been a long sojourn*
> *When will I return*
> *That's my one concern*
> *To Grön?*
> *I yearn for Grön*
> *Oh how I burn, &c., &c...*

A proud youth, the blackest of the black, the most flatnosed, thick-lipped and frizzy-haired, him of the most outlandish aspect, Mekkech, stood at Johnson's elbow, hammering a bone upon a copper disc. "Shall we get out?"

"Don't you think we will?"

They looked at each other. Johnson drew a shrill sound from the pipe he held at his mouth.

"What are you going to do?"

"I'm going to have a big dinner. What about yourself?" Mekkech was silent. "Have dinner with me, old chap."

"I'll see. Perhaps I'll come by after dinner."

"Come after dinner then."

Mekkech went and sat down by himself.

There, his back bent, gazing at the metal disc he held gripped between his knees, the strange fellow tapped and banged away, frowning, absent, unhappy; Johnson watched him. What, he asked himself, had he to do with all this? He was hungry.

Outside, crowds were treading and stumbling over

stretchers, punting musette bags, first-aid kits, regimental reading matter baled in five-kilogram bundles, kicking medicines and the articles of war and what not this way and that, abusing the wounded, plucking off their dressings, belaboring the maimed with their own crutches, wielding traction splints, assaulting the nurses; fighting amongst each other, disputing the spoils, stampeding when whistles announced the approach of incoming trains, clambering over the carriages and locomotives, it was an orgy, they coupled and swooned on the tracks, men had dropped their trousers, women had raised their skirts, some stood fierce-eyed, trembling, others stood hollow-eyed, masturbating, some hooted and jeered and lynched betimes, laughed and wept, bit and spat, dashing out into and back from the Place des Philosophes where the fountains, floodlights, music were all turned furiously on and where an occasional airplane crashed. Men identified by buttons pinned to their lapels, insignia reading "Union Leader", "Shop Steward" or "Trustworthy Syndicalist", sent their flocks trotting out to meet the élite guard who, twirling their batons, afoot and on horseback, stood waiting for them, grouped in the most various formations. Alongside the coaches, the extravaganza was maintained at a steady boil by the liberal admixture into the press of paratroopers and guardsmen and security beserks who now feigned mutual enmity, now composed their differences and cooperated straitly. Missiles of every size and description whizzed through the steam, the soot, the smoke; turbines exploded; sheds and switchtowers were ablaze; members of the Youth for Cleanliness movement were pulling up rails and hurling roadbed. Coffee mugs, sugar bowls, an expresso apparatus from the third-class buffet penetrated into Lieutenant Johnson's coach. Panic on the platforms, in the waiting-rooms, near the baggage depots and, of course, although out of sight, on the great square where there were amplified skaters' waltzes. Water gushed from split pipes, a string of boxcars burned. The combatants were many fewer after midnight and by one there were only briskly scrapping soldiers and, circling round the knots of contest and digladiation, were squads of old men supporting propaganda on laths and broomsticks, paper and oilcloth banners for the most part demanding more pay, a new offensive, increased outlays for national defense, discriminatory hiring practices, less housing, and an end to food subsidies. Viewed as a whole, the spectacle was vulgar.

So it appears in the telling; to a young man—I was twenty at the time—it was the highest adventure. I had completed my training; my unit was readying to sail. As yet untried, full of zeal, eager to be off, we were called to the terminal and directed to take a position between two élite battalions. It must have been at two, or a quarter past, when we, munching candies or chewing gum, saw Petitcon descend from the coach; Johnson came next, his company followed in single file. While Petitcon fired left and right, Johnson drew up his men. "Head for the main f'ck'n' exit," Petitcon cried; Johnson repeated the command; they lurched and swayed towards us. Elements of the élite battalion on our left moved out; Johnson's company angled; their manœuver was frustrated by the precipitous intervention of a powerful group of élite which swept in obliquely from the right; we saw placards bobbing up and down, sinking, disappearing; a small shell detonated; everyone began to cough;

the conscriptees staggered, veered, and those who were able to, ran—ran shamelessly—; the company was irreparably scattered, stragglers were trod under foot; it would have gone very badly with them had not the roof covering the platform collapsed at that crucial moment; we fell back, were ourselves divided, and I found myself with Johnson and a handful of his friends cornered in the men's toilet, presently awash. At least a score retiring guardsmen backed towards us; attempts to close the door failed; there was an abominable crush; I saw Johnson lose his footing and fall through a partition and into a cubicle occupied by a man who, with an oath, clearly beside himself, rose in a fury from where he had been squatting. The dim light at last revealed those familiar features; I gasped, something caught in my throat, I believe there was a lump there, I felt as if I were about to cry; it was weakly I added my voice to theirs:

"Avenging Tiger!"

"All hail to His Excellency!"

"Monarch!"

"Phoenix!"

"Atlas!"

"A marvel of a man!"

"Nulla ferant talem secla futura virum"—Johnson's erudition lifted itself from darkness and difficulty.

"Supreme Product of Humanity! Spouse of Nature!"

"Lamp of the World! A long and glorious life to our Commander!"   Space was cleared; Claude-Maxime strode out, through it, and was gone. Paralyzed, I lingered there.

While heralds and couriers, the military and the secret police dashed hither and yon, beat about the station, tootling their whistles and flashing their badges, ranged the circumjacent streets and combed the ruelles, scoured the square, nosing out whomsoever of Company B of Regiment C of Division D of Army E was in a living and ambulatory state, Lieutenant Johnson lay in the jakes, meditating.

Meditating, yes, certainly, for he was down, and being down, unquiet. This well-seasoned young man... what a world of difference subsisted between us, I who was just embarking upon life, he beneath whose feet —now trapped amidst débris and held vertically in the air—the vessel had foundered; owing perhaps to my intense excitement, the blood pounding in my arteries, the blood I had seen spilled, my admiration for him, despite his posture, exceeded, I own, all bounds; at this moment, as I too reflect, as I look back upon it, now, as I write, certain of those sentiments return to me: I am still able to see and wonder at the calm of this well-seasoned young man... who, when in a disadvantageous attitude—and he had been uptilted not a few times—was accustomed, not to brave heats, fencing with his fingers and sudden stirring in order to translate himself from an aleatory into a positively fatal situation—for no one attracts blows like the resolute and upright man—, but to adopting a mood of thoughtful complaisance. Slothfully, perhaps, womanishly, if you like, cravenly, I will allow, Johnson was wont to bend his finer attentions to problems of policy. Even in his earliest years, those who were charged with schooling this independent personage remarked, quite apart from or rather as a complement to his great vigor of mind, an inaccessibility, a protectiveness which may be the jewel of an exquisite constitution but have no lustre in a leaden scheme. Some declare this refluence the product of egotism, others attribute it to timorousness, still others to haughtiness, to melancholy; now what is it they are in a sweat to condemn? what is it their sweating condemns? Only when one is prone may one discover the meaning of abuse, accomodate oneself to it, outlast it. Johnson —herein abode his genius—was at his best when at his least, when things went worst. They will exclaim Johnson was blessed with no magnanimity, was little, hollow, a waste within, ashes, dry dust, death, humanity's contradiction, not a man but a statue, a painting, a graven image in a blighted landscape; then bow yourselves not down, or do as you please, but not as did that lady Beatrice who, captivated, so she persuaded herself, by his adolescent charm, his delicate features, his dreaming expression, took him upon her breast, touched him, framed in marble, touched not him and knew not what to do but say he would be much sought-after and there would be many others who, also, would not know what to do, what to call him, how to act; and therefore, she had said, accident would pursue him, the lightning would intend him; and she fell asleep, exhausted, no, she pretended to sleep so as to convince him, or herself, she was truly spent, because she wished to be, but not he, not spent, not for nothing. And so this is nothing to you, poor dear boy? Woe unto you, poor much beloved Samuel Johnson, hard times and many trials lie ahead. It is not that you have had some kind or other of culpable beginning, or not entirely that. It is the glory of God to conceal a thing. The glory of the king is to find it out.

There, lodged amidst the putid papers, immobilized by the disposition of beams, plywood, plaster, his neck clamped between porcelain and toilet seat, the latter anchored by the castiron water tank a lunge for the chain had brought crashing down, there, in the offensive gloom and humidity, he did for a space deliberate. To what effect ? To none immediate or clear. For his mind, usually vigorous, was presently dulled by the pain centered behind his missing eye and diffused through his head, his limbs; and his ideas, thus, were driven off the definite road, changed into impressions that strayed at random in the champain beside.

They halted upon a desolate scene divided by a view of the ocean. Dunes behind, cold bog and fen, decaying tamarisk trees and wind-sawed pine and stinking tall grass for middle and fringe. Closer up, six or eight score boys with daggers and a few guns, his schoolmates and himself, huddled in clusters, nauseous and maculate. The sea was scummed with oil; two thousand meters from the shore sat a derelict careened on a bar. The sky was like fogged mica, many times thick, now luminous, now opaque as the smart wind riffled the leaves of cloud and mist. They were just come home. They had waded to native soil at daybreak. Kelp tressed a shattered oar, a broken boat skittered on the shingle, waves came gently in, like mechanically advancing stairs. They were that morning landed, and had not done more than shake in the feral light that was penumbrous this minute, glinting the next. Some crouched, some crept about on hands and knees, some were still, others lay flat, only a few talked, and then in a whisper. One of his companions stalked the wandering oar, seized, flung it far out into the water; he saw slanted eyes; the sly waves sent back the oar, it reared itself, that oar, and dealt a crooked face a blow, smote a little head, a casque rattled off as a strap broke, blood flowed from an open mouth. There were peasants among them, in dark coats and trousers, wearing string ties about brick-red necks, peaked caps, barefoot; then the boat scratched crabwise, fullswung scythes and mattocks battered it, splinters figured Samuel Johnson as a slender young man, disguised, his head buried in an outsized rusty helmet and with an enormous filthy bandage for a visage.

An electric torch's beam followed his twisted body; he saw us the moment we saw him. His single eye glowed cherry-red. "Get up," said a guard. "Come along, Samuel," said a dark-skinned person standing beside me, "we've got to hurry," and he put his hands in his pockets as a second guard aimed a kick at Johnson's back. The eye did not blink. Then Johnson laughed. "I can't move, I'm pinned," he explained; "inform that oaf." I would have intervened had not the person beside me observed: "It was sooner or later." "Don't be absurd," Johnson shot back, and laughed a second time. The guardsmen lifted the water tank, pushed the plywood aside, picked up the beams, tugged Johnson free and jerked him to his feet. "Well, Mekkech," he began, "I have been thinking." Mekkech made a face, his lips thinned over his teeth, he seized his friend by the collar, squeezed with his small hands; "Wake up, Samuel," he urged; "be alive." His voice shrilled. "We're going to eat and drink and dance and sing." Then he spun towards me: "Get along." His eyes were moist.

I felt suddenly embarrassed. Then I grew angry. These were mad dogs, corruptors, disease-bearers, they were perverse. I sensed the limitations of my twenty years. I was jealous. But I had orders, privileges.

Fortunately, I did nothing. The guardsmen, paying no attention to me, led Johnson out. He walked along, overcome with weariness, or disgust, or pain, or sorrow, he went obediently with them. It was his principle to cede.

Petitcon had marshalled the vestiges of Company B in an uncertain line; Johnson took his place. There were scowls of defiance, muted consultations, looks of foreboding and dismay; I was convinced they were monsters. Strangers had been dragooned to fill a hundred vacancies. His sleeves rolled up, Petitcon paced to and fro, bawling like an exorcist: "How about a little smile there? What's the matter, are you shy? Chest out, get your f'ck'n' chests out, legs straight, keep your f'ck'n' feet together, pull in your guts, stop that f'ck'n' mumbling. A little f'ck'n' pride in your outfit, what about some f'ck'n' *esprit de corps*. You're going to a party. Recreation"—he was perspiring, it was a very warm night, he had probably wounded twenty people and killed a dozen—"and recuperation. Button those buttons. Stop dribbling, sonny. Somebody wipe him."

Off they tottered, no very glad picture, the halt leading the blind, lowing, gurgling, whimpering, heedless of the Captain's admonishments, shivering even in that ripe, luxurious night; 'twas, I knew, a band of thwarted assassins, noxious funambulators shocked out of their unclean tricks, now puling and whining and shedding the most crocodile tears. "Whup, whup, whup, whup, whup," shouted Petitcon, "whup, whup, keep in step, whuppetywhup." Staggering, reeling, they strayed chaotically down the short avenue between the Palace of Justice and the Accuser's Palace; when abreast the latter, they sent up a few insincere

salute , a tremulous caterwauling. "Once again!
Three f'ck'n' cheers for the Jovian Eagle! the Tiger
in the Jungle, the Superintendent of Wit and Learning!"
And so on, till they were gone from sight.

⁎

A version of subsequent events was provided by
the Objector; his evidence, if that word may usefully
describe an hysterical tirade delivered in very bad
faith, was broadly as follows:

After a hazardous passage, led by Petitcon, Johnson
and Mekkech, Company B gained St Bridget's Fields
before the night's seventh hour was much advanced.
Everything was prettily laid out for the warlocks'
sabbath. There was a great fire burning, an altar
set up, benches and tables were put around. There
were plates and cover, mugs and glasses; kegs of ale,
flagons of red and white wine, burgundy, hocks, chablis,
Côte de Beaune and Sancerre, armagnac and cognac
brandies in demijohns. Fruits lay in baskets: fine
Normandy apples, oranges from Spain, apricots,
grapes and peaches, currants and granadillos; cakes
and pastries and puddings were next to them; meats
steamed in pots, boar and game—pheasants, grouse
and wild turkey—turned on spits; by each plate there
were flowers and linen; a delicious aroma rose from
this plenty.

The veterans arrived, were wonderstruck and fell
upon the mid-summer sward.

"Very nice," said Johnson. "Now what?" "Better
raise Satan," Mekkech advised. "I?"

"Who else? You have authority?"

"Shouldn't I clear it with Petitcon?"

"Petitcon's left.   You're the chief."   So they began
to croon and howl, their regards fixed on the declining
moon, and to intone:

> *"Lalle, Bachera, Magotte, Baphra, Dajam,*
> *Vagoth. Henneche Ammi Nagaz, Adomator Raphael,*
> *Immanuel Christus, Tetragrammaton, Agra Jod Lai.*
> *König! König!" etc.;*

their wicked sacrilege remained unanswered.

"Well?"

Mekkech suggested they try another.

Off they went again:

> *"Amion, Lalle, Sabolos, Sado, Pater, Aziel, Adonai*
> *Sado Vagoth Agra, Jod,*
> *Baphra!*
> *Komm! Komm!"*

and ended with a shout. They were famished and
in earnest.

"See there," said Mekkech.

"Very nice," said Johnson.

The Devil bade them make music and praise his
name.   There were rude instruments at hand, similar
to what had been supplied them in the railway station.
They blew upon small pipes; the droning sounds
delighted the veterans. They became jovial. One
soldier bent over a horse's skull strung like a zither;
there were sonorous horns and drums and more gongs
and cymbals; some seized up cudgels and began to
beat the ground. Faces became flushed. Meantime
the Devil sang hoarsely, through his nose, producing
a roaring wooden sound, very loud; the whole fra-
ternity shouted and bellowed together.

"Enough," said the Devil and directly began his
sermon. Fair and dulcet was his perfidious speech,
his manner was gracious. "Be not afraid," said he,

putting out his hands and gazing upon his followers; "spare not to eat, drink and be blythe, taking rest and ease, for I shall raise thee up at the latter day gloriously."

Johnson was seen to sip from a glass of black wine, then touch his lips with his tongue.

They all knelt; the Devil distributed black bread and sprinkled a dark, sweet liquor on his young worshippers; did his work with solemnity and rapture too, and the infinitely corrupt, the doomed to fire were appeased, had no mind of their hurt, none of the iron in them, and tasted not bitterness but a false joy, awful for the deception.

A kid goat was sacrificed; blood flowed from its throat upon the earth; the Devil summoned three of his faithful, Johnson was one chosen and he went forward, and they tore the kid in pieces—yes, the Objector insisted, the kid, in pieces, and these they buried in distant parts of St Bridget's Fields.

"Keep ye my secret," said the Devil; "be ye silent; now be merry."

One and all, they fell to eating and drinking most gratefully. Johnson procured two roast grouse sizzling from the fire, and a bottle of Musigny for himself, another for Mekkech, whom he looked for and failed to find. Mekkech was not there; Johnson called out his name, asked to left and right, had anyone seen Mekkech? What had become of Mekkech?

They had not but begun their dinner, had only taken their first mouthfuls, when John Stearnes, his cameramen and legal aides, his bailiffs and his virgins arrived with fierce whoops and halloos. Flashbulbs sparkled, resistance was crushed, and a creditable capture was made.

The Objector concluded his plea with a flourish of

characteristic unintelligibility. Although he would never cease to oppose these atrocious farces, he said, sniggering, he had given up attempting to understand their purpose; by which he meant that their inspiration was obscure and imprecise: if, as by its criminal nature it rightfully may, the State thirsts for victims, just as its machinery yearns for employment and its essence passionately desires a real and satisfactory existence, if, granting these fundamentals, why, the Objector wanted to know, why must these futile and preposterous ceremonies (here Johnson raised his hand, more or less halfheartedly seeking to make himself heard; he was ordered to hold his tongue; a smile appeared upon his face and he went back to reading his book), must these futile and preposterous ceremonies, the Objector repeated with a sneer, which demean rather than exalt, betray and deny rather than confirm, continue to deprive the organism of its vital aliment? We are, he cried, indulging in the most cynical practices; however, we are working counter to our interests; I for one am no pessimist; I for one have faith. Despair? I? No, not I, etc...

Strange motions? Necessary proceedings, my heart. Those bludgeons and bayonets, those lashes, those fists, those feet, that firmness, that decision? Precautions, Aimée; this keeping of the peace is no children's game. The security of the State has its own sublime mathematics. Some we hear say it is purposely esoteric, impenetrable, inconsequent, a spectral nonsense, and altogether capricious, a formal abracadabra, much shape and sign and no substance. Why, they ask, are not the laws spelled out in the country's native profanity and then graved on some material, something durable, and publicly exposed so as, doubtless, those monuments, of which we already have too many, may be oggled at and pissed upon? Why, they ask, perfectly unaware this is no age of simplicity, why is it we have many laws, many lawsuits, many lawyers? why, worse than no counsel at all, counsel appointed, no speech to be had from your advocate unless he is further fee'd? that, or he is as mute as a fish, better open an oyster with your teeth; and when he lets loose his tongue, he gibbers like an ape, will not be stopped, says too much, far too much, brings on every kind of danger with his prattling till you pay him to say nothing. If, as you hear them say, there be no jar, he can make a jar, out of the law find still some quirk; then it's begun again, years pass before the cause is heard and when it is determined, by reason of some miscompture, oversight, hindsight, trick or error, it is as fresh to begin fourteen years later as it was at first; a lawyer grows old during a suit, he is so busy here on earth he will plead his client's case in hell. Citing the ancient complaint, they say that he who goes to law holds a wolf by the ears, or as a sheep in a storm, runs for shelter to a briar; if he prosecutes his cause, he is consumed, if he surceases, he loses all; where is the safe ground here? what's certain? He that buys a house must fill it full of writings, they go on; deeds, papers, contracts, quittances, maps; there are so many circumstances, so much is upon condition, relative, there are such repetitions, so many words, variations, shades, hues of particulars; but no document is so accurately made by one that another will not be able to find a crack somewhere; one word misplaced and it's all annulled, worthless, ha! see there, my good man, this means nothing, you're a victim and a dupe, keep a sharper eye next time, that's my advice, what a pity. That which is law today is none tomorrow; what is sound in one man's opinion is very faulty in another's; whereof, they say on, we have unnumbered litigations, unexpected seizures, sudden entries, daybreak embassies, inexplicable disappearances, no person free, no title good or almost good, but only bad in some degree, and the least degree suffices; we all dwell in a limbo of perturbations and delays, of forgeries, heavy costs and incessant alarm.

There, I've given their argument in full, it's in print; see what wild stuff it is. Can these be the reasoned criticisms of any person that has had experience with our courts or our police? A very seditious note rings through these inventions; seditious, divisive, incendiary carping, from beginning to end. What's this mightily, patently fallacious allegation, that our justice is too slow? Or does it come from the mouth of him who thinks not to benefit from a prolonged hearing? Is our law truly labyrinthine if our justice is speedy? Or is it that a contentious guilty fellow, who must borrow fantasies already three centuries old, makes a very unsteady course on the contemporary road? Our laws are mysterious and shifting? Not to a right-thinking man, not to a mind put in willing harmony with the State, which conforms with the general will, Right and Reason incarnate. There are some born for the rope, you know and so do they, and it is they who, even in the cart or upon the scaffold, stammer and cackle indifferent rubbish about bronze tablets and plain-worded codifications; they hang with illtemper and protest on their lips, exclaiming, even as breath runs short, that they did not know. *They did not know!* A patriot, ready to follow his leader anywhere, is a man who knows, in the right proportion and the correct amount, and above all he knows when not to know; it is instinctive with him; you'll not hear a good citizen moralizing inopportunely, making diatribes, bawling about civil liberties, reading out of the constitution and reciting schoolboy lessons on the field of war; this State is not maintained by scholars and comparers of texts, we are not much in the debt of critics, editors and specialists in fiction; let not our patience be taxed, you walking universities and holy men, full of proposals for amendment, points of order, heresies, remedies, abnormalities, scandalous imaginings, special readings, revolutionary writings. No, it is not amongst that crowd of loutish drones and scavengers we find simple honesty or respectability; of the two, the professor and the common man the professor likes to call uncouth, it is not the simple-minded fellow we hear saying well on the other hand, perhaps, it would actually seem to me, the thing is to be conceived, although by no means sure I venture to point out, maybe, and tradition informs us. There are none of those cant phrases in his mouth, which his superior common sense bids him keep shut. 'Tis a rule with us: an absolutely fallen angel put the apple in our ancestor's hand; a good clean man is able to resist temptation; he needs ask few questions; he bends before God's law and perfectly well appreciates ours. For the law is preventive, inhibitory, its force is negative; it does not construct or create, it aborts, it destroys, it undoes when it is invoked; what else would you have it do? What is this criminal jargon about good laws, benign laws, lenient laws? You want no laws at all... ah, my friend, mend your ways; far from beholding the city of man born on earth, you will fail of attaining the kingdom of heaven.

On the 7th of August 19—, Samuel Johnson stood on his own two feet in the prisoner's dock; Judge Porn presided; the court-room contained, apart from his honor, the accused, a clerk, a recorder, two guardsmen with particularly uninteresting faces and a submachine-gun apiece, and the Objector, who had brought along a well-charged briefcase, who could not sit still, and who said:

"This is nauseous. By which I mean to say that it turns my stomach; although I have never ceased—"

"The man is how called?"—Porn opened the trial.

"By the name of Samuel Johnson," answered the clerk, a great hirsute, bulky man, swart and angry.

"His age?"

"Twenty-eight years, my Lord."

"Parents and kin?"

"None living, my Lord."

"What does he do?"

"My Lord, he spies birds and reads the condition of things present and the probable cast of things future from their flight: from the direction they take, the hour they pass overhead, their grouping, how high they fly, how fast, and in what numbers; he augurs, but pronounces no prophecies, caring but to know, not to announce, is close and deep and single; he studies to improve himself and, though young, is learned in a quantity of arts and sciences, curious lore and trivialities, all manner of diversities gone out of fashion; *omnifarium doctus est*, yes, at this little age, and has a reputation among scholars; he is a great gastronomist as well, but not hospitable, being of a solitary lone-dwelling temper."

Johnson's expression, as he listened to this characterization, manifested his approval of it.

"With what is this prodigy charged?"

"With warlockry, magic, sacrilege, uncleanliness, blasphemy, rebellion, conspiracy, my Lord, and murder."

"What evidence of witchcraft?"

"His silence, my Lord. The Devil has sealed his lips. As well, much authentic and sworn testimony and the Indicator's infallible intuition. Finally, these photographs." The clerk tendered Porn two portfolios. "He led the sabbath."

"When?"

"On Lammas, my Lord. He was taken in St Bridget's Fields with one hundred sixty-seven others, in the act."

"And of murder?"

"One of his noxious band was slaughtered at the feast, my Lord, by his command, he having government of the revels."

"And eaten?"

"That is not impossible, my Lord."

"Disgusting," interrupted the Objector, spraying his throat with an atomizer.

Porn gazed at the prisoner. The prisoner gazed at the ceiling. A pause ensued. The recorder waited. The clerk scowled. The guardsmen stroked their campaign ribbons. At last, Johnson emerged from his reverie.

"Very good, very good," he said; "carry on."

Tears of mute anxious laughter rolled down Porn's chubby face. Johnson looked at the judge in surprise.

"My Lord—"

The Objector had begun to speak.

"Enormous, inexpiable though this man's fault may be, there is yet a necessity, a bond that subsists between him and ourselves..."

Porn blenched. A man of many and shifting moods, he grew sober, grew rigid; as when walking in the mystery of the forest at night, stealing through wintry darkness rich with the promise of possession, exultant, his nerves quickened by the glorious stars' pressure, a hunter will feel the trap's steel bite, but understand, and not cry out to the unhearing solitude, realizing it was he himself laid the snare, realizing the chase has ended, that he has become a poacher in his own domain.

The Objector pursued his way.

Constructed out of that clown's hired vehemence, articulated by drollery and bought rhetoric, Porn, looking through half-shut eyes, saw the nightmarish difficulty materialize, and suddenly remembered the levantine tale of that phantom spirit transformed from vapor to puissance by rubbing, and an esoteric word. No, things are not so simple. They have, precisely, double edges; there is also the secret, the darker side of things; an appalling complicity unites the hemispheres. In this world of tyrants and their prey, the mighty exact what they will and the feeble grant what they must, to be sure; and yet there is a bond... that makes the master, helpless, acknowledge his dependence upon the slave and, that all their wishes and dreams may come true, consent to exchange estates with him. Resignedly, endeavoring to do so cheerily, Porn uttered the only possible answer:

"Then let him live a little."

Well now, here was something few would have anticipated: an act of mercy, an act of generosity, an act of cunning too ; oh astute Porn, was it then that, in a stroke of sudden seeing, you perceived you also were on Grimoald's list ?

.

"I am getting older," said Puddick to himself. It was his birthday. He was twenty-nine. No one knew. He had received no gifts. He climbed the twisting marble staircase, cooling his moist hands on the stone. Mirrors on columns and walls reflected at least fifty Puddicks. He stopped to look at one. It looked thirty-five, in a certain sense, seventeen or eighteen in another. The whites of the eyes were clear, but the hair was dull and thinning, the tongue was not coated, but the mouth had gone slack; "I'm a marked man," thought Puddick, retreating.

It was to the Accuser's heart they were careful not to allude during their afternoons together.

Puddick took his place, inhaled, and was ready.

"Fourteen years a riveter—well, well, now isn't that odd? There you have it: everyone making his contribution. No work, no food. No work and no food. He was in the shop where the nacelles are fitted about the engines. Nacelles—you didn't know? I dare say you had not the faintest idea—it used to be done the other way, your Grace, I say, your Grace. Oh, are you there? I say it used to be done the other way: they mounted—it would be more proper to say, they inserted—the engines into the nacelles. Then what do you suppose happened? You haven't the faintest idea. Tut. Of course not. Ak. The supply of strategic materials slackened—dwindled might be preferable—and they had to devise a new system:

Mother Necessity! However, mark you, your Grace, note well that it was all for the better. The present system is immeasurably more flexible. The bottleneck has always been in airframe production, not, would you believe it? in engines. But what was I telling your Grace? I have it: fourteen years, or very nearly. Excuse me, but I do find it queer. Very queer. Ak." Puddick squeezed shut his eyes; his head ached; he opened his eyes and was sad. He looked forlorn. He massaged his temples.

Their smutty conversation picked up again. Puddick hoped that it would soon begin to do them good.

"Anyhow, be that as it may, the stamped aluminum sheets are brought in—by some kind of mechanism, wouldn't you expect—they're ingenious, oh, clever. Bottlenecks, shortages, ak, nothing will stop them." He raised his eyes, squinted, waited until there came to him, through twinges of migraine, an image of aluminum sheets swaying from the foyer in the direction of the salon, shimmering, rippling beneath a conveyor belt. "I've visualized it," he announced. He glanced at Yvette. She was absorbed with her chemicals, her fragile little vials, eyedroppers, spatulas. "And meanwhile," said he, "the engines are on the test blocks, turning over at—confound it, the bleeders—forgive me, your Grace—what do they turn over at? five hundred RPM, a thousand? I've no idea. Too fast to perceive, hence to count, with the unaided eye. There is an electric device they clamp, perhaps they bolt, indeed they possibly screw, probably clamp over the propellor shaft: it is called the tachometer, from ταχος, swift, and it supplies the deficiencies of human vision by counting, electrically, the rotations, which are rapid, you may be

certain; it does more: it is capable of detecting flaws in
the propellor, if flaws there be, and sometimes there
are, our perfected techniques of propellor manufacture
notwithstanding: this instrument has, marvel of science,
the properties of an ear, the human ear... but not, however, the appearance. The rhythm is recorded on
a screen, interpreted by a green line... pulsations, oscil-
lations... now, I believe there is a certain gadget they
use on human brains—"

"What's that?" demanded Yvette. She was reduc-
ing some blue crystals in a small mortar. Her wrists
were slender, her fingers long and tapered, and they
leapt; now she added a fluid, now a yellow powder.

"Why, to determine whether the patient is insane."

"Patient?"

Puddick looked up again, weighed his words with
care: "For every patient," he reasoned, "you have an
agent... But I'm drifting, drifting." It had been
in a self-assured tone he had rendered the fierce rite
of manufacture—he was able to distinguish the sacrifice, the libation, the invocation, the instruction. No,
he admitted, there were others, less well perceiving
than he, of a different sensibility, who saw less in these
industrial procedures than might a bard of the machine
age over whom they cast a spell; Plant Eleven was,
for him, for Puddick, the theatre of the most dramatic
events and emergences. The noise of the machinery,
the taste of the air, the tense inclinations of the shop-
workers, the glint of steel, of copper raveling in a coil
from a whirling mass, of slowly advancing chisels,
sudden transpiercing jabs—he had discussed each
element with the voice of authority. Puddick's twenty-
odd long novels had won him a reputation for realism,
for clear-seeing and toughmindedness; as he had drawn

the picture, there had been a certain virile grate in his voice—Yvette was fond of it—, especially when he had come to the perils of engine-insertion, the too rarely sung daring of workmen who used electric riveting hammers in the neighborhood of aviation gasoline. But now, as he watched her roll her poison into pills, he dropped his eyes, intimidated. "Ah," he said. Perhaps, he thought, it was less whimsical than it had at first seemed. He went on in a subdued voice:

" 'Dr Samuel Johnson'—I am quoting the report —'Dr Samuel Johnson, *honoris causis*, has completed thirteen years, eleven months, seventeen days of penal servitude. He has been steadily employed in Plant Eleven, Engine Installation, and will be enlarged today, without other recompense than the abbreviation, by thirteen days, of his original sentence, and the heartfelt thanks of his country his industry has served with such devotion.' "

"Really!" cried Yvette, beginning to chew one of her pills, "that's a howl."

"Curious prose," Puddick remarked, studying the text.

"It's killing."

"That's not all. They have a great deal more to say about the man. How odd. Fourteen years— might just as well call it fourteen—; I was a mere boy then." Slack though he knew it to be, his mouth was also sensitive; it trembled; he lifted the clear whites of his weak, beaten, intelligent eyes; there was much poetic unquiet in his breast as he considered this difficult Yvette—this restless, rapacious woman who had raised him from dust to celebrity as the State's most influential author, foremost among the seven hundred. "Oh yes," said he, his voice now shrunk to a whisper, "yes." He descried what he flattered himself was his fate... depending tremulously from the rice-plaster ceiling: where rose-skinned damosels jibed their lace-arrayed young seigneurs. Ah, he thought, what a curse is self-consciousness; then said, aloud: "The murderer."

"It's like fiction," said Yvette, "your fiction."

"Yes," he assented. "It seems so real, so much more than real. Oh, your Grace! wouldst that we were not so lucid."

"I remember reading," Yvette began, grimacing as the pill began to take effect, "about a magician, I think, who came from a wealthy family, a young man who lived with a lot of stuffed animals or pet fish—"

"Birds, your Grace. Stuffed birds," Puddick said wearily, certain he would soon lose interest. "You were a girl then and I was a..." and his thoughts, quite as he had foreseen, seemed to disintegrate, to become separated one from the other, such was his lucidity, his self-consciousness, lost, as in a forest. He beheld himself as a mere boy; a little boy lost, a very small, a very vile little chap, lost, unlistened to; he was on the verge of tears, such was his intelligence, exhausted in that emptiness and dark, marked. He had had the sensation, observed the scene before; he folded his hands.

Yvette's were nervous. She was thinking of her age—it was definitely that she was thinking of—and of her figure, and broke a second tablet in two. "Stuffed birds"—she ran it down with a swallow of water —"coming out of prison. When I was a girl? You say coming out? or going in? It's like a book." Puddick reminded himself she seldom read. He watched her closely. She appeared troubled. He had a feeling she was frightened. Something told him so.

He rallied for a moment. He imagined that she too was concentrating her most precious attention upon the past, yes, the past which, in her case, was not a forest but a jungle, not an emptiness but a space too densely crowded, teeming with all that quickens the blood, starts the nerves, arouses the senses, a realm not of stillness but of infinite movement, wherein the self is not supreme in sovereign loneliness, but consumed by sovereign excess, denatured by the effects of a supreme indifference characterized by gleaming stripes of chromium casting a thousand partial images, gusts of bubbling carbonated water, sweet deceiving food, candies and creams and syrups; this was not the forest of scarcity and alienation, this was super-abundance and obliteration; no, he thought, that should not have suited him at all. He could picture a curious mood for which ennui was not quite the term he sought. There was grief behind this resplendence, the grief not of passivity and senselessness, but of energy expended forever, hopelessly. Perpetual, unthinking movement; well, Puddick decided, that also denotes the hand of God. This woman was bound to become the object of a cult. He saw it, how could it escape his eyes? Within a golden aureole, dynamism, drama, and startling paradox. How awful, how wonderful: the dramatic career, the dynamic woman. "How sad," he said aloud.

"Don't feel sorry for yourself," she retorted.

Puddick felt a lump in his throat. She must be miserable, he thought. To his alarm he saw a wave of gaiety sweep across Yvette's exquisite features.

"Chéri," she murmured with the sudden, unpredictable tenderness that never failed to penetrate to his very bowels, "you're always causing me bloody frights—but this damned claptrap—"

"Coming out." Puddick held his ground doggedly, glumly. "Can they possibly have planned to have it happen this way? It doesn't make sense: why put him in if he is to come out?"

"It's all a bad dream. We'll have him popped right back again, won't we? Then we'll wake up."

There were choking noises from an adjoining chamber.

"Claude-Maxime, your Grace... the Accuser wonders whether it will do an ounce of good."

"Does he?" she snapped. "What does he care about doing an ounce of good? Do you think it ever does any good or any harm or anything else?"

"His Excellency asked me those very questions this morning," said Puddick, "when we read the report together. Ha, ha. A coincidence."

Her eyes shone. She swept her chemicals aside. "And what did you say, my little squirrel?" His reply was barely audible. He visualized her canonization. "You said you didn't know? You should know, you two," she pursued, half rising from her chair; the angle at which her head was inclined cast a shadow beneath her eyes; "and if you don't, my little Puddy dear, you shouldn't let people know you don't know."

Puddick flapped his hands. "There's no telling. After all," he suggested, "there could be several Samuel Johnsons; for instance, there was the lexicographer. His works are in the municipal library. However, he lived in the eighteenth century. Ak."

"Stop it," she warned. "They're all the same. It's always been the same thing, the same man—"

The Accuser's oaths traversed the thin partitions.
Puddick took heart. "And the same problem,"
he rejoined. "It's never been solved and I don't
think it ever will be. Do you want Grimoald to have
him put to death? Do you think Grimoald, any more
than Porn, any more than anyone else, wants to put
him to death? Why, no, nor do you, and you're quite
right. We're not here for that. Where would Johnson be then? Out of the way; but that's not at all
where we want him. They must be punished, that's
the first thing," said he, gathering momentum; "to
punish them they've got to be alive, present, accessible,
not utterly out of the way, but nearly, that's the second
thing. And the third thing is, punished for what?
If it is something they have done, that thing is done,
and punishment is useless, it is weakness—or it ceases
to have its old, original usefulness, which was exemplary; but do we wish to give examples? surely not;
do we wish more or fewer violations of the law? are
we not the law? must we not be opposed to exist? I
put the question this way: can we exist alone? Does
not our increasing strength tend to crush opposition?
are we not hence obliged to encourage opposition,
subsidize it, yes, set up the pins for our bowls to scatter?
is that not the game? is this not a game? So we punish
them for something they have not done, or for nothing,
or for doing nothing—we are on dangerous ground
now, for do we not create something, and every time
does it not prove to be something unpunishable...
unimaginable... or only imaginable and impractic-
able... all spirit, all essence, all absence, but all crime?...
I don't know what to call it; I don't like having to
give it a name, it is enough to imply it," said the novelist, wiping the sweat from a brow whose height his

receding hairline emphasized; "we've given up trying to find a title for it: crime has no name. Does that effect anything, however? that is what you want to know. No, my God, surely not; our difficulties are not over; we punish them all the same, at random, as best we are able; I tell you, it is difficult to govern. We punish. But why? For what purpose? I'm not asking you for what reason—we haven't got one, we don't require one—but what does this game *get* us? Ha!" cried Puddick, raising a finger, presenting a chewed fingernail, "it gets us laughed at. Do you... eh, understand, your Grace? Do you see where this is leading us? No, never fear, *they're* not laughing, because they're in no position to laugh; *we're* in power: *we're* laughing," he said solemnly, "and who is in a better situation to laugh? That's the queer thing, that's what's odd, to realize that—it's very serious, very complicated, and it may be altogether new. Great God!" he exclaimed, impassioned, "the earth has started agape, there are come out of this sphere's fiery entrails a host of..." but Puddick quickly took himself in hand, and continued: "we're behind them, I tell you: they have an advantage over us, it's measured by their weakness, and there's no closing that gap; they're tricky—they may not look it, but they are. It all worked so nicely when we began and when they were ignorant of the resources they have since learned to exploit. It used to be so simple. Do you remember? We were children then. We frightened them. They took it very well. Everything seemed possible. But what's to be done now? They're afraid, they're gorged with fear, they're so afraid, they've been afraid for so long they're accustomed to it, that's been their diet, that and hunger, and they've had a surfeit of fear and now they're jaded and now... it bores them."

"It bores me too, chéri."

And presently they had more bellowing from another room.

Yvette went to calm the Prince, and to dress for dinner.

Puddick was left to greet their guests; one of them, whom he knew only by name, had risen swiftly, he had heard; Puddick knew not what to expect. There was a smiting of arms and heels at the Palace gate below; a black figure was hailed in the smoky light of cressets, and the watchword was shouted down vaulted cinderblock corridors whose marble sheathing had been five years on order. There, in a minute, stood the swift riser, a tense irritable little man, made like an iron arrow, with bitter eyes; they made a lasting impression upon Puddick who later affirmed under oath that "they belonged to one risen from the dead and he had a mouth that was once full and made to smile, to speak fair, to hold the soul, now withered by the gall that is tasted below." Puddick did his polite best; said His Excellency and Her Grace would join them shortly; would the visitor be seated? Mekkech, for it was no other, was restive, his behaviour made the writer uncomfortable: "Though we are not acquainted," Puddick observed, "our work, which, I take it, is similar, had sooner or later to bring us in touch," and the desolating retort he had from Mekkech for the time being forbade further attempts. It was an uncommon day that was ending: a day full of death and derision; had not the earth split? this man seemed to have emerged from the chasm. He had, Puddick knew, an obscure employment, which in itself was upsetting, was one of Yvette's favorites, which prompted

feelings of jealousy in the nation's number one novelist, and had been away for an age, which was against
all the rules.

"I dare say you're delighted to be back," Puddick
proposed. This time Mekkech said nothing; he
tramped up and down before the immense masonite
fireplace, scuffed the heavy crimson carpet and disengaged quantities of wool, scowled when his toe drew
a hollow ping from the massive andirons. He peered
at the Louis XIV clock. It had stopped. He lifted,
rattled it, put it to his ear, then muttered in digust
and restored the clock, ungently, to its place. At
length he moved to the tall window and stared morosely
over the city to which a Christian government had
brought, as they say, the odor of sanctity.

Puddick blew his nose. Catastrophically, the day
perished; the ceremonies began. They were in answer
to a mighty yearning and in the nature of an attack:
a superbly coordinated, a devastating, a thrilling
spectacle staged by the authorities, by those who were
the most far-sighted, the best qualified. Flights,
squadrons, wings and groups, whole air armadas and
air fleets rush whistling hither and thither; scores,
hundreds of airplanes of every description fly in every
direction and at every altitude, according to a scheme
the specialists, the planners are in a rage to perfect;
in formation and singly they dip, bank, roll, spin,
race like comets in the fortnightly show of force, now
and again colliding in midair, some bursting against
the sides of buildings, others upon the pavements,
in the fields... Even the most indifferent are roused
by the performance, the blasé are such no longer, for
a tense hour complacency is banished out of Grön:
its masters emerge from their funk, their minions

cease for a brief term to sulk; objections fade from scoffers' lips, fear gains an object, love is rewarded, belief fortified, even souls of mud are in an ecstasy: thus are we fed, a glory animates our visage, our body is awake. Rockets, harmless tracer shells, a few armed projectiles weave a web in the purpling sky, search-lights make it glisten, a fever is in heaven and earth. Phosphorous and magnesium flares hang swaying, floating, exuding their watery incandescence; it rains like balm upon Grön, transforming the city into an undersea grave in whose deeps bones, pebbles, stones, relics take wondrous inflexions, are curiously limned and blent in remarkable patterns of furry shadow and flat grey-green; the world seems to toil through its own phantom; the echo of its shout deafens its own ears; storm, lament, query dance deep; objects are displaced, are broken, spoiled, cindered in a flash, whelmed, and are joyous. A hail of steel fragments sweeps roofs and thoroughfares; the hail thickens to a deluge as ponderous transports and gaudily decorat-ed bombers spill things of continually enlarging bulk —tins of fuel and auxiliary wing tanks, then chunks of armored plate hiss, at last beams and telegraph poles and a miniature locomotive thrash through the aqueous air; certain among the younger pilots are allowed the extravagance of a few hundredweight of incendiary compound.

"Wild, isn't it?" Puddick said during a moment's lull.

Wilder still was the low-level drop of an airborne division, seventeen thousand happy-go-lucky youths of tested valor and boundless zeal. The manoeuver was accomplished with exceptional precision and negligible losses; in the disorder that ensued, the survivors—impetuous, mettlesome lads!—gave themselves over to committing many of those deed upon whose strategic and educational value only the accounts of generals deserve attention. The observer beheld no more, however, than the swift, as it were effortless subduing of a weak-willed defense: among other things, this had the sharp flavor and acrid odor of mock warfare: the resistance put up by the irregular battalions—composed of housewives, disabled veterans, the unemployed, die-hard teams of adolescents whipped to a frenzy—excited only a normal degree of contempt. Grön was secured—delivered—in a trice; there were the customary incidents of playful give and take as the liberating invaders avenged their comrades; the night watch replaced the day; the air force thundered off; and from within public shelters and countless damp little retreats came the shrill notes of the national anthem, brave song rose from the breasts of nearly a million grateful people.

"Extraordinary people," Puddick reflected.

"Helots," Mekkech announced.

To Puddick, the routing and skoyling, the fireworks, the fatalities knit themselves into a unity whose significance was religious and whose effect was medicinal: a potent aspirin; he felt instant relief. A sigh escaped his lips, a smile settled upon them, he shook himself. "That," said he, "is one point of view, oh yes... but this—"with a broad gesture, his second of the evening "—this, you'll find nothing like it in any other country. It is difficult to imagine what it means to us... equally difficult to express what it means to them... or how much money... thought... labor... and sheer daring have gone into developing what we have just seen. Those games—"he trembled"—those games spring straight from the nation's essence, they correspond to our deepest desires. They are a symbol, a metaphor —but this is not something that benefits from an effort to understand it. It occurs twice a month. Every two weeks—hard to believe, isn't it?" Scattered fires burned, were put out, went out or went on all over Grön. Children watched the molten tar congeal. Billposters completed their work. Ambulances rambled unhurriedly towards the outskirts. A natural gas reservoir burned, blew up with a cough. And that was all.

"Have you had an agreeable journey?"

"I have an appointment at half-past nine," Mekkech replied. "What's keeping them?"

"Oh, my. Dinner will be served soon. I appreciate your eagerness to see His Excellency and Her Grace and they shall doubtless be most content to see you. Are you enjoying your stay in the city?"

Mekkech remained at the window, looking out at the smoke, contemplating something for which he made no effort to hide his disrespect. The by now faint caroling gave way to faint moaning. "Happy population," said the agent. Hands outstretched, groping, supplicating, a blessed however guileful and somewhat sinning multitude fumbles towards its bed to curl up, quivering, in a final goodnight sweat of gratitude before sinking into the sleep of mercy. Silence, broad and profound, the echo and sleeve of the elusive metaphor, lifts itself above the blackout and that shroud enshrouded sits the vigil; an honorable, hard-earned peace, an anaesthetic calm are sovereign here; from a bathroom come an old warrior's wheeze and the sounds of water struggling in pipes.

"A tricky bunch," Puddick repeated.

Mekkech fell to cursing.

"...so many lunatic beasts, I'd say," came above the twitch and jerk of water; then Claude-Maxime, several rooms away, his blotched noble face pushed against a shaving mirror, his little red eyes running with rage, began to gargle.

"One feels like a fool, a fool," thought Puddick as he listened to Mekkech's unfamiliar accent:

"Lop away a chicken's head, and the bird may live for hours—"

"The war is going well?" Puddick interrupted. "I take it you have been in the East? What good fortune! Personally to observe campaigns whose cost, intricacy, and length declare the righteousness of our determination and whose continuance gains our arms the merit no victory can assure: for great acts are not in the issue but in the doing: enterprise is its own reward: we seek no riches on earth: blessedness is the gift of heaven."

"—for years, perhaps, who knows? Granted the necessary care and circumstances, it may go on scratching dirt, stalking and strutting and shitting in the coop, laying a perfect stream of eggs, hatching broods; loving, increasing, questing, feeding; having no concern nor need, save to be eaten—wasn't this supper scheduled for eight?"

"But," Puddick cried, "they need it, they want it."

"What are you talking about? the new breed of headless chickens?"

"We have polled public opinion, polled it again and again—"

"Johnson must be charmed, the poor old rotter. This is entirely in his line."

"—they can't do without it."

"No, I dare say they cannot."

"Nor can Johnson," Puddick affirmed, "since you

bring him into the picture which is, frankly, precisely where he belongs. I'm pleased to hear you mention him: he's been on my mind, as a matter of fact we've all been thinking of him. He's being treated very leniently, you know, too leniently according to a prevailing opinion. Certain harsh realities have got to be driven home to that man; he has shirked his responsibilities—I don't care how well he managed in jail; he's out of it now: he has his privileges; he also has his obligations: his first duty is to give evidence of some humility. He must face the truth. No, no, I beg your pardon, call it vulgarity, call it what you wish. I tell you he belongs to them; what you have just seen is therefore his as it is theirs; that's what you tend most conveniently to forget. Well, you've been away: you've forgotten. What a pity. I understand you. You fail to see it. We did not impose it, it came from them, and to them it is precious, it's all they have—perhaps," said Puddick, becoming aware of a rawness in his throat, "there's been some mistake. It is silly to quarrel. I don't enjoy quarrels. I believe in reason. I am sure you will adapt yourself. It seems to me a matter of rehabilitation." He stood up; he sat down quickly, blushing. Mekkech, he realized, had said nothing and was now wearing a crooked smile.

A shadow of his old self, the Marvel of a Man, the Jovian Eagle entered the room supporting a decanter of brandy. The glorious old invalid promptly slumped into a chair, set the crystal decanter on a lacquered coffee table, covered his face with his hands, and bled slowly from a cut he had given himself while shaving. "This evening," he prophecied in a blurred voice, "is not going to be a success."

"Your Excellency, our guest—"

"I saw him. Tell him to be gay. I won't have any moping. Can't afford it." The Superintendent of Wit and Learning poured himself a drink. "Well, where's my reliable Lechecul? Has anyone seen Lechecul? My God, you look as if you were spectators at a wake."

"Our guest," Puddick resumed, "says he has had a comfortable and uneventful journey, and that the city exceeds all his expectations."

"Damn it," Claude-Maxime roared, "what's the matter with the man? Has he just lost his best friend?"

"As for this evening's air-games, your Excellency, he finds them—"

"Staggering, aren't they? Too bloody much for me. Well he's here, I've seen him, he's in damned fine fettle, apparently very firm in the kidney. That will do. What? He's going to stay? He's come for dinner? Too bad, too bad, he'll regret it." Claude-Maxime coughed, puffed, choked and spat. The Objector was introduced. "Ah, Lechecul! Just in time, my boy, these idiots were putting me into a stupor. Well, sit down there, sit down; isn't this hideous? How are you? I've never felt worse."

Puddick frowned, then pulled at his earlobe, then fell to work again. He enjoyed speaking: "The Accuser is in capital health," he said, "but even constitutions as vigorous and youthful as his have their limits imposed by nature. It is a wise man who does not press himself too far or too hard, but observes moderation in all things." "Not bad, no, not bad," said the Objector. "Where did you get this droll fellow?" Mekkech demanded.

Then Puddick noted that man is the measure of all things and began to crack his knuckles; he pursed his lips and went ahead: "His Excellency has had a trying day. Few of us could hope to engage the problems, shoulder the responsibilities with which the Accuser has incessantly to cope. Even we, whose burden, compared to his, is so negligible, even we are practically at our wits' ends, at the end of our ropes—" "He's never done better, upon my word," the Objector remarked. "—yes, burning the candle and the midnight oil at both ends with this prodigality. Nothing new," the author of at least a dozen *romans fleuve* hastened to say, "there is nothing new under the sun. Just more of what is substantially the same until there is no differentiating between objects, between object and subject, all puts on an identical look, a common face, oh it is a deathly visage you see in things and in men, the interior sense is shared generally, an universal amalgam, a lump is formed of particles and details that contend no longer, swoon, I tell you, into uniformity, one cannot distinguish past from future; everything's at a halt, the present is an eclipse, or a hiatus, everything seems old and banal, one feels oneself snared in a machine, turned into a machine indeed, a machine that repeats and repeats a monotonous but sacerdotal function." Puddick's face had turned scarlet. "Births, deaths," he expostulated, "deaths, births: on and on. But I rove. That," he pointed out, "that is government for you; and that is being governed—"

"But, you know, that stuff is ready for the typesetter," the Objector whispered to the Accuser; the latter belched; and a stunning, emaciated figure discovered itself in the doorway. It was Yvette whose charm, half the product of nature, half the effect of pitiless maceration (fasting, exercize, regulated vomitings, enemas, she had tried them all, none had failed her, the results were breathtaking), had her bent double; she clutched her stomach: Puddick sighed: his avid gaze appraised soft golden brown skin, yellow hair in magnificent coils, sunken cheeks, a slender neck ribboned by unusual tendons—all this luxury in a saffron gown tailored for a wraith. "Mekkech!" and she was about to embrace the grim little agent when from between her clenched teeth there burst that shrill cry that had captivated the greater part of Europe.

"Cramps," Puddick explained, gone limp with admiration.

They went straightway to dine. Was it a festive reunion? Were there served, as in former times, a wine of Grenache and roasts, veal pasties, pimpernel pasties, black pudding and sausages; hares in civey and cutlets, pea soup, salt meat and great joints, a soringue of eels and other fish; roast coneys, partridges, capons, luce, bar, carp and quartered pottage; then river fish à la dodine, savoury rice, a bourrey with hot sauce and eels reversed; next, lark pasties, rissoles, larded milk, sugared flawns; finally, according to the old chronicler's recipe, pears and comfits, medlars and peeled nuts, hippocras and wafers? or a sumptuous fish dinner, to wit: pea soup, herring, salt eels, a black civey of oysters, an almond brewet, a tile, a broth of broach and eels, a cretonée, a green brewet of eels, silver pasties; salt and freshwater fish, bream and salmon pasties, eels reversed, and a brown herbolace, tench with a larded broth, a blackmanger, crisps, lettuces, losenges, orillettes, and Norwegian pasties, stuffed luce and salmon, in that order; followed by porpoise frumenty, glazed pommeaulx, Spanish puffs and chastelettes, roast fish, jelly, lampreys, congers and turbot with green sauce, breams with verjuice, leches fried, darioles and entremet; then dessert? Did they eat all this strange stuff? Can you seriously ask such a question? Do you think our austere habits are show only and that behind our professions of temperance and simplicity of manners we are monsters of hypocrisy with nice palates and great guts, proclaim one thing and practice another? Accept my word for it: this meal was frugal, not patrician, it was no bacchanal, there was no sickening luxury here, no riot, no debauch; on the contrary, there was a climate of depression in the room. Claude-Maxime spooned his soup with caution, studying his plate; Yvette chewed a piece of knackerbröd. Gossip and prattling, boasting and swearing—one heard very little of that at these State suppers. Yvette asked after Mekkech's paintings. "Paint?" said he; "I don't paint; I've never had a brush in my hand." "Then sculp, you do something artistic, don't you, carve, whittle?" "I don't sculp, I don't carve, Madame, I don't whittle." "You're a grump tonight," Yvette chided. Mekkech and the Objector exchanged sneers. "I always look for ground glass," said Claude-Maxime; "I never find it." "But how could you hope to find it? It would be invisible." "That's right," said Claude-Maxime, "it would be impossible to see." "Furthermore," said the Objector, "it would sink to the bottom." "So it would." "Therefore, my advice is to ply your spoon with care; above all, don't eat the vermicelli." "You're quite right," Claude-Maxime agreed, "I mustn't do that. But what if it were not ground glass but a stimulant?" "In liquid form? That would be impossible to detect save by taste or smell, and if tasteless and scentless impossible to avoid," the Objector explained; "a sip, a few drops would suffice." "Right you are," said Claude-Maxime, pushing away his plate. "How could I get on without you?" They relapsed into silence. Claude-Maxime blew his nose into his napkin. "Tell us a story, chéri," Yvette commanded, "amuse us." Puddick started off on the one tale they relished, the only one he ever told, the only one he really knew. "Once, when we were in the jungle," he said, fixing his eyes on Mekkech, "there was a hunt..."

Figures and motifs, memories and demonstrations passed through his mind. "A man had escaped, fled off into the jungle, you see, in flagrant violation of all the regulations, and he was wanted, although you must understand that when I say he was wanted I mean it in no ordinary sense. Want, under such conditions, within an alien perspective, want..." An incomprehensible mess, he thought, and conquered an impulse to burst into laughter in the face of the destruction. Innumerable pages were one by one despoiled, torn one after another from their insolid binding, confused by some accidental, barbarous hand, then crumpled, crushed. "The fugitive's name meant nothing to us; but when we learned his description, when they mentioned his disfiguration..." Puddick was once again astonished when the remorseless fingers uncurled and exposed so little lying, defunct, in the palm; that minute blob of matter, grey in color, had been transpeciated by the grip from vegetable pulp into what seemed half putty, half meat, and that was why it seemed to him suitable to place the action in the jungle, and to have a man take refuge amongst the consuming plants: the essence to which he was sublimated was, he conjectured, instinct; he resisted another temptation to laugh. Whenever he recited his story, there would flow into him, who was so much of the time dry, the realization, gaining him like a tide as the story advanced, that he was a person... a person: there, over there, was himself, Puddick, and here, elsewhere, everywhere else was what was not Puddick; he was an exclusive entity afloat, subject to use, but the core of him was insoluble... Mekkech's black eyes were looking hard at him and their effect was to make him hard to look upon. "Now," said he, "the problems wherewith the pursuers were faced were these..."

By ten, Her Grace's and His Excellency's sedatives had put them sound asleep. The Objector's round face had a rapt expression. Puddick was well within the jungle's depths, tracking his quarry, drawing nearer to him, scrutinizing signs, sniffing the air, musing upon a spoor, a clue; "Yet we sought to keep our distance; we had only an intimation of whither we were being led." Long before Mekkech had got to his feet and blown him a kiss, the thing was gone far out. "We had been too long on the trail. There was no turning back. There had been no warning, not a single hint..." Jungle tools in hand, chewing quinine and betel-nut, sneaking between vines, Puddick was surprised at nothing unless, now that he was a person, at his apparently complete willingness to accept, to bend before what, by George, looked like a personal fate; nor had he any regrets, not a single regret. "The fact is," he said aloud, "I'm really a young man. But I feel tired." He yawned. His chin resting in his cupped hand, the Objector drowsily regarded the young man, his face shining like a red moon.

Part the Third :

OLD FOLKS AT HOME

Dr Samuel Johnson had surrendered his machinist's kit, his goggles and his gauntlets. Everything was checked and found in good order by the foreman of the section, Serafim, a broken man. Every step in his twenty-five years of gradual breakage had been marked by a promotion. And so the least fit was the most important man in Plant Eleven: Serafim had been decorated again and again. The wearing of worker's medals is compulsory: although idle, casteless, conditionless, Serafim had learned to wear his with that kind of resignation of which, in Johnson's opinion, a man might be proud. Peering narrowly through the corrosive haze of oil vapor and exhaust fumes, Serafim returned Johnson's 100-obol deposit and said that it was all grist for the mill, eh? In the blue ruinous fluorescence of that no man's land, Serafim's teeth, used by a decade in some allied power's lead pits, jumped like dots on soiled dice. Johnson, for whom the cripple represented just what the system paid him to represent: an ideal specimen of the worker, never ideal save when invested with authority, never ideal save when bastardized or orphaned, made conscious of his responsibilities and a leader of other workers, hence made an almost proprietor, a virtual holder of shares edged by God's own gilt, made privy to the secret answer, instrumental to the suppression of the question and the maintenance of the workers' wellbeing, their silence, Johnson, I say, respected Serafim, for he was a sufferer. And Serafim responded to

Johnson's sympathy; he too could divine and be amused by paradoxes and infinities and he knew just where the line is drawn that demarks the beginning and end of the alliance between the besieged. "For a philosopher, time, no matter how it is spent, is never lost; no effort is in vain"; from his, Serafim's viewpoint, it had been a pleasure. "In the main, synthetically considered," said Johnson, "it has. You have succeeded in making me feel I belong here, you know. I'll not forget it." Ceremoniously, having exchanged some further remarks of no great interest to those who care little for the problems by which workers fancy themselves intimately affected, they shook hands and bade each other a tender farewell. Then, at gunpoint, Johnson, who sensed he ought at this critical moment to be fully aware of what he was about, to be informed by a veritable sea of light, to be squared evenly against all his human possibilities all come awake, Johnson walked further into the trap.

Once arrived in the chaplain's office, Johnson asked: "What have we here?"

The room, or cubicle, measuring twelve feet on a side, was furnished in very good taste: walls hung in dark red velvet, in one corner stood an altar, between two perfumed candles a stylish, brand-new copper-plated crucifix, some prayer-making gear and books and beads, receptacles for storing the host and sacramental drinks were within easy reach, an oil lamp hung from the ceiling, there were no windows, the air was renewed by electric blowers, an expensive rug covered the floor, one chair, a prie-Dieu, was placed in the center, under the lamp. The chaplain, a lad not three weeks out of the seminary and smelling still of the movies, sat on the floor, beside the prie-Dieu, his legs squeezed

together and tucked beneath him, his full pleated
gown spread in a circle; he was smiling kittenishly
or blissfully, his back was arched, his eyes shut. Ah,
but he was nothing if not charm, gentleness, infant
sagacity, unspoiled deliciousness itself! He raised
his eyelids and met the Doctor's cyclopean glance
with confidence; he tossed back his head, opened
wide his little mouth, pink, made to speak loving
words, sweet exhortations, and spoke, with a ravishing
display of little white teeth, of the past, of the future.
From the folds of his gown he drew a scroll tied up
in a ribbon. "May thou go forth a new man," said
he, dilating his little nostrils and darting provocative
looks at the sinner.

The Doctor took his certificate and produced, in
his turn, an amiable smile, and with a touch of nostalgia, no more than a hint of nostalgia in his voice, said
that, after all, perhaps they were right and it is seldom
one changes in any fundamental sense, merciful heaven.
The small priest shrugged—or it may have been that
he quivered—; it was clear he didn't care a damn
whether they were right, for he knew how they came
by their opinion, and he pouted. Silently, Johnson
besought the protection of his gods-in-hiding. But
the priest had sharp ears. "What was that you said?"
"I have the habit of prayer, Father," and Johnson
submitted to his embrace.

Panting, the boy drew away, cocked his little head,
adjusted his chestnut curls; despite his disorder, his
voice was controlled and he spoke as if he were having
to do with a foreigner, taking great pains to enunciate
clearly—and with what an enchanting effect! "May
thou go forth a new man, my son. Know full well
and take comfort: no mortal hath the right or is so

situated he may reproach thee thy fault; not one amongst us is absolutely unattainted; error is our part, we are covered with crimes; thine hath been expiated with dignity and humbly."

"Tush," murmured the prisoner. He retrieved clothes and belongings confiscated fourteen years before; he made a quick search: of his money, he discovered not above half missing and felt more at his ease.

"...faith, hope and charity," concluded the little man of God, radiant, advancing his small white hand; never was skin so soft, never veins, fingers, nails, line or flesh's tint so delicate. Johnson bent, turned the chaplain's hand, kissed it; then left the jail. It was six o'clock.

Freedom, he noticed, weighed lightly upon his shoulders; resolved not to become its dupe, he picked his way carefully down the empty streets. He was in the St Andrä quarter; the perspective was bitter. The prisons lay behind, factories and warehouses spread to either side of him; between buildings were wastes, lots overgrown with the uglier of the unusually small number of plants that are able to grow in Grön; abandoned excavations, gulfs heaped with rubble, brick, fills, weed, pools of stagnant water, mounds of ordures, objects derelict and decaying amidst which were domiciles: shacks, huts built of bottles, gasoline tins; and great chipped billboards announcing that it would be on this site model homes might perhaps rise. All this desolation breathed, was a giant infected lung. It occurred to the free man that the nether myriads were not to be forgiven their tenacity, that deformity and ugliness are, as the ancients believed, close bound to natural wickedness. Away, away!

he thought, have done, 'tis enough, give over or get out, you have stayed too long.

He saw he had got off to a bad start and tried again. It was hard to know how to make this fresh beginning. His hand had been forced: they had literally expelled him from prison, had they not? Fourteen years below ground surrounded by common men harmless because held well in harness, he too well in check, like them waiting, those common men and he, waiting passively through what, in a sense, one wished might be an eternity, with petrified hope waiting to release their tiny explosions of energy, but terrified by the thought, not wanting to do that, to go off valiantly in that smothering infinity of privation; for what then? it was the one possibility: to get out: and then? the waiting had become of greater and greater importance. There had been no mistaking it. When he had asked them, their reply had every time indicated they thought of the prison as a sanctuary. Here, on the surface, he smelled the presence of famine. "We have our work," they used to explain in the underworld; "what have they got outside?" They hated words, of course, but their hatred was honest. He had watched the rise and fall of their chests, it had been so still there below he had sensed and been dizzied by the thudding strokes of life in their bodies, the negation baffled by four thousand beats every hour, down there, in the shadow, where one could see very well; where they watched him. And so long had he kept sealed his lips there was a deathrot in his mouth. At first he had been afraid to speak; then he had given it a try; finally he had given it up. He went about his musing scientifically—dead men, men practically dead, can dispense with passion. Fourteen years of watching them and

being watched: every muscle and nerve keyed to anticipate the possible crisis that might be unleashed by
someone's unreason, to foil the thrust of chance tensing
in them all; his annihilation, his feeble dying self face
to face—in cells, in the shop, the mess, the gymnasium,
over the bucket of slops, by the air vent when at night
lust would put them on their feet and eyes starting
from their sockets they would pace two yards east,
two west, two in the other direction, again two in
another, and fall down with a gasp and lie without
stirring until the bell rang—, face to face with their
apparently inexhaustible raw strength glinting through
rags of common mute flesh, through their poor common decency: watching a common goodness that,
unmotivated, might at any instant deliquesce and
against which for defense he had only stealth and
craft; he had been busy in jail. He had watched
beside the tubs of paraffin, in the prison library, while
they ambled about the basketball court, while they
took their showers together, he had watched at the
little puppet theatre and when a warden had given
them a lecture on pollution; and always the pernicious ounce of enduring mortality in the heart of this
dungheap a-dying. At first he had thought of getting
out, for he had been in his twenties—had indeed kept
on thinking of it, but in a steadily changing way.
Next, observing no improvement, no relief, he had,
in his thirties, decided he might be destined to remain
there forever, as it were, and to go on smouldering
always, existing always in the anguish of continuance.
Finally, entering his forties, he came to fear lest the
spell be broken, lest any sudden decision be taken;
he ate more slowly, his pulse slowed, everything he
did or thought was done or thought more deliberately,

with increasing reserve and often after extraordinary preparation, if it were an act, and long periods of preliminary meditation, if it were the formulation of an idea. He seemed to notice the same development in all the others. They became more solid, more sober as they became older. The longer he knew them, the less familiar they became. Nothing grew clearer with the passing of time until, like them, he would fix his attention and dwell for hours on end upon undistrainable, mysterious details: a spot on the floor, a faulty condenser, a cartoon in a picture magazine, an excrement in a pail, his hair, someone else's hair, genitals, teeth. He thought he understood what this evasiveness manifested: as each of his mates aged, guilt composed itself in his visage. This you were forbidden to recognize, at this you had, as a brother, to look. The worst of it all, the especially condemning part was the rock-ribbed imperative of cleverness, of deceit, of treachery, of going inwards and inwards to keep the peace and preserve the enmity, until you were a pariah asneak in your own foul essence. That amorous little chaplain was right: inconstancy works hand in glove with the beating heart: it is all infidelity and meantimes there glows a livid, angry coal, the spark of life sunk in flesh's trash and litter.

And now look at yourself, see what you've turned into, look at your own image.

Johnson could do no better than this. Ruefully, he admitted how poorly he had kept his faith; it would be too much to request that the gods, themselves in trouble, make allowances. He had not been fifteen minutes at liberty when he had realized the worst: all hope of pardon had disappeared; what in the

Devil's name was he to do now? There they went, the hopes, rising buoyantly up, like droplets of steam or like the little winged figure that departs a body with the life fled out of its mouth; he was not far from death. But he was getting no nearer. He and the others were cordially at swordspoint: neither his doing nor theirs, but thus it was, or appeared to be, some grandiose ordination had made it so: cleverness, deceit, treachery, those were the devices, and he had adopted a defensive posture in the ludicrous belief it well became him to provoke no damnable byplay. Thus he had masked his helplessness and flattered his vanity, saying, it shall not be Johnson who gives offense, who slays the peace, no blood on his conscience, he was set upon murderously and did aught but preserve himself as would, as must any idiot, none of the fault rests with Johnson, good old Johnson! righteous Johnson! etc. ah! poisonous fantasies, diseased confections! dreams and justifications more dangerous than outright slaughter, reasonings more wicked, more perverse a thousand times than the blind unapologizing assassin's brute act and anger. He had begun with sweet denials and pampered himself with soft words, striving to evolve a seamless ignorance and then to paint it with the mild colors of innocence: for example: how slight is the degree of control we possess over the anciently cast design of things; or: a melancholy fate, this one, of compulsory crime; or: how absolute and absurd is the empire of chance, 'tis all kill or be killed, better with hard laughter on thy lips to die in a manly condition than to be shorn of dignity, stripped of all that bestows credit... Thus, he had started as half an aggressor: he had begun by composing a black account of tensions and animosities, he had begun by bleating the vulgar complaint. Necessity and reflex were large in his mind, they soured his stomach but flattered his weakness: unlimited, he found, were the means wherewith to forgive anything provided one first reduced oneself to nothing, and, dear oh dear, he had found there was nothing to that trick, no indeed, the world was full of little shortcuts and aids, ever means was valid, that is to say false: you need but resort to one and the case against you is secure: you are thoroughly the aggressor. Johnson beheld the flames. In fourteen years' time, the ornithologist and heir, the leader of men and the captive, one-eyed Johnson had acquired a perfectly symmetrical perspective; he had lived with others; had been dying with others. Presently, he walked abroad, confused by his term, wisened by it too, strengthened by his new skills but deprived of his smooth silhouette. What a strange fellow they'll think me, he said to himself. I wonder how I shall manage; I wonder if I'll have to make myself understood, and will that be possible? Knowingly, Johnson put one foot forward, then the other, stepping further into the general snare. He had re-entered the Nation.

There came a rush of wind, a flickering of lightning, thunder boomed feebly, down fell a torrent of rain: a fit, a spasm and that was all, the god too had done his best and was spent; Johnson heard the drone of aircraft.

He was struck by the memory of fourteen years of noise: the whirr of ventilators, incessant roar of motors, smash of presses, grate and cry of abrasive wheels. At large, glancing about him, he listened: nothing stirred in St Andrä: the last drip of water, the divine semen of impotence falling upon unresponse, the growing wail in the sky; but, in the city, nothing.

Grön was submissive, in it he was alone. Underground, the manufacture of what would wipe away the atrocity, destroy destruction, the manufacture of hope weapons surged tirelessly on, but in the midkingdom nothing surged, nothing spoke, nor moved, nor seemed to hope or be.

He felt no strong emotion. The season for that had passed. He had come dry from his confinement, there he had left his manhood, perished there, he believed, were his desires, consumed in pathos, the pathos consumed, smoke finally and the smoke dissipated by the wind, swallowed up by space. He was tired and he was dry, but otherwise felt tolerably well. It is not every evening one is released from prison, he said to himself, experimentally; and observed the phrase to fall lifeless, null, upon his heart. Several more paces, then, to himself, he framed it again: It is not every evening one contemplates a fourteen years' term of exemplary behaviour in jail, for an offense one never really committed; and again noted the utter indifference of an organ which, he had read, he had heard, had been told over and over again by excellent authority, was articulated so as to resound to bold, clean strokes of this kind. But (from a different tack), but they freed me before my time was run out; they were not obliged to; I should be grateful, perhaps, obliged for this act of cruelty; but I am not; why did they let me go? how much of me did they set free? how can there be nothing left and still something that knows the rest is gone? He felt pleased with himself.

The same wind returned, 'twas now very soft, and it held the evanescence of the man, irreclaimable. Dr Johnson deigned to look at the sky, he looked with compassion upwards at that limitless greed, his regard considered the original whore for whom he had no more desire; he looked at night's flux, circuit, music of stars, at the immense obscenity, the last, surely most sordid of industry's creatures. Had he not been long in the cave? and now he was out through no fault of his own; and what was his situation? he was aghast at his thoughts, his language; and now what relations obtained between him and the others? was he to melt into a weeping delirium? shed tears of civism, enter into a fit of joy? were his rights restored to him? priceless treasure! and his duties? Ah, a free man's duties! He was sensible of the plight of his kind, he was sympathetic, towards benevolence he inclined; everything in due measure. Of that plight, because it is common, overspreading everything, everywhere, evidently unchangeable, evidently a principle, he who had changed had come to recognize there is nothing to say whereas formerly he had simply not known what to talk about. Even, he thought, even if that plight, his and others', cries itself aloud, and it is apt to, it is nevertheless, and by reason of its vociferation and insistence, something upon which to be silent. Silence—would that not be doing his best? He almost thought this evening worth fourteen years in prison.

The evening wind, laden with his discarnation, also carried remote sounds of collective lament; ha! said he to himself, those well-trained choirs were tuning up for the concert. From isolated points came, now, a few squeaks of private rage, a few gratuitous squeals; they were finding their tongues. He sniffed: there was the same heavy odor of putrefaction, prosperity and progress, the dependable, nearly-but-not-too-human stench. But he was firm; for he was naught.

He passed several late-January wrecks, others dating from February, still others declaring a fatal springtime, each placketed with a terse relation of the event; here and there were little piles of bones, or sprays of artificial flowers, cheap iron wreaths. This evening, the entertainments were concentrated in a western sector of Grön. Posters and informations were glued everywhere, evidence abounding of the prodigal hand, the bold concept, that complex luxuriance wherein, grained proximately, interwoven, were the jubilant temper and somber statements like: "Man achieves authenticity before death" and "Herewith the glory that surpasseth understanding": papers wherever the eye rested, printed sheets bright and crisp, some fixed above roasted citizens, some detached and serving as cover to what, lo and behold! were individuals perishing of inanition. Johnson, fourteen years out of touch, appraised the news. He laughed good-naturedly. He felt hungry, and quickened his step.

Anna Wickenzipfel opened the door and flung wide her arms, sobbed, shrieked, was beside herself with joy, surprise, and so forth, emotions which puzzled the Doctor, for he and Anna were unknown to each other. "But I've heard so much about you," she explained. Still the Doctor kept his distance. "Now, now, my good woman," said he, "enough, for this will lead to grave disappointments." "You're just the same," she gasped. Picture it! She hardly knew his name. Why, she hardly knew her own. "Really?"—for Johnson was not one to overthrow the kettle, swamp the boat—, "really? How kind of you to say so. And you've not changed either. Stand back there, let me look at you. So. Quite as I thought. Do you suppose," he asked, lowering

his voice and carefully entering the flat the dear departed Adrian had leased for him, "do you suppose, on this
short notice, you could prepare a large dinner? For
you were a heavily talented cook, if my memory does
not fail me, or if my information is correct. Those
are two ways of saying the same thing, my good woman."
   She was staring slackjawed, being an artless personage. "Did they convict you?"
   "My goodness, yes, you can be sure they did. A
copious dinner. Duck—*canard à l'orange* or, what would
be yet more appreciated, pressed duck, do you know,
and find me a Rhone wine, a 1904 label, it would seem
to me, with..." and he made out an exhaustive pres-
cription; to which, he knew, when he had concluded
a speech whose mere delivery did him a world of good,
she had not listened. "In brief," said he, "do your
best." "So you've done time," she breathed, a look
of what he had to interpret as craft hastening towards
her moist eyes. "Mind what you're about, woman."
He closed the door and demanded: "What is your
name? I mean to say, I have forgotten your name."
Yes, just as he had foreseen, she hesitated as if she had
forgotten too, then rallied and said: "Anna."
   "Anna," Johnson repeated; she nodded. "A fine
name. I am going to call you Anna. Never fear,
we'll be fine friends. Even were your name Jonet
or Isobel or Goody or something like that, we'd make
friends, Anna. Mistakes have been made before.
What counts is the last word. Forgive my chattering.
I haven't had such a nice conversation in fourteen
years. And, tell me Anna, how is it I find you here?
You say a gentleman sent you here to wait for me?
Exactly. And you've been waiting a long time?
Yes, of course you have, ever since I left, and it must

have been very dull indeed, just as it has been for me. And during this interval, Anna, you have been all by yourself? I see. No young soldiers, you say? Have there been any callers? Any mail?" Anna stuffed her fingers into her large blue mouth. "Why," said her master, "have we then to start with reticences?" Johnson glanced at the brass tray lying on the table by the umbrella stand, and at the card lying upon the tray. "So it's Anna, is it? Simply Anna. Ho hum diddly-dum. Anna, Anna, Anna, curious, I don't make anything of it." He dropped the card back on the tray. "Whereas this other name, the one on the card, has a distinct effect upon me; it evokes a certain response, how shall I phrase it? The response is inward, secret, you cannot see it, don't bother to look, Anna, these responses are not to be seen. Nor are you to concern yourself with what lies outside your province. Run along, my dear," the Doctor sighed; "I'll dine at half-past eight. That gives you at least two hours. Do your best. Anna."

"Duck," whimpered the maid, and fled.

It is not every evening one returns from fourteen years in prison, where one has been, unjustly it would appear, unfairly, inequitably, despotically confined for having killed a man one might have easily, but probably uselessly, maintained one did not kill; confined under extremely difficult circumstances, those of unceasing anxiety, perpetual alarm—but we have given ample space to all these difficult circumstances. The reader is either convinced or is not convinced that life in prison is disagreeable. I only wished to say that it is not every evening, after a quarter or a fifth of a lifetime, half a generation in prison, during which the earth has thirteen times circled the sun,

many a star has died, many another been born, one
returns to a strange home to find one's alleged victim
intends to pay one an after-dinner visit. Dr Johnson
decided to acquaint himself with the premises. He
walked into the room outfitted as his study, containing
all his old belongings. He made a rapid inventory
of his stuffed birds; on tiptoes he assured himself Anna
was busy in the kitchen, then dashed back to peep
quickly into his filing cabinets, at his books, and again
at his trophies; the desk, which he came to next, seemed as he remembered it; his papers were there, the
same pen lay uncapped, the contents of an open ink-
bottle had evaporated to black dust.

He sat down and collected his thoughts: these he
felt ought to be focussed upon the problem of being
as much as possible, and for the short period allotted
him, the new self that had surfaced after an ordeal.
He sought for an appropriate attitude. That was,
he realized, after itemizing all that had been done
for him, the one thing he needed. As for Mekkech,
"He will have to apologize. For I have been grossly
imposed upon, have had great expenses, been ill-used.
It could have been fatal. The wonder is it wasn't.
The wonder is I may have benefitted from it. But
I have no choice: there must be an explanation. Yet,
what can he say? Will his apology be for being alive?
It is chiefly for his sake I shall demand an explanation.
For his sake? Has he been subjected to churlish treat-
ment? is he unhappy? Has it been then to kill him
because I did not kill him? But was it ever in my
power to prevent this crime that was never committed?"
He could not keep off a smile. And so this was what
being at home was like! He poured himself a drink,
sat fondling this chin of his he was to keep uplifted,

then started to write a report. "Dr Samuel Johnson, *honoris causis*, has completed thirteen years, eleven months, seventeen days of penal servitude. He has been steadily employed..." He glanced at his fingers, the torn nails, a few healed cuts, the dark grease wedged into his pores. "If, then, anything is possible—"

Johnson took his place, Anna served him; her step was heavy, definite and percussive, like the trampling of an army en route, and for a few moments the Doctor was afraid lest her presence trouble his digestion. He began, however, to reconsider. To be sure, she possessed no great elegance, was not overly refined, in her look, stride and impeded speech the ordinary predominated, it seemed unlikely that lofty thoughts were often in her head. If Nature had lavished her favors upon Anna, they were not superficially on display, no, for she was of a rude composition, powerfully made and a little at haphazard. The Doctor had, as we know, a prejudice against vulgarity; he distrusted what is not bounded by polite restraints and systematic circumferences. The essential outlaw, he held, is nothing but existence insolid tending constantly to volatilization, nothing if not the threat of change from an uneasy state into nothingness' tranquillity; upon all bodies play the universe's negative pressures, he would reason, and what is unstable yearns to be fetched out of shape, longs to be metamorphosed, to proceed through atrocious mutations, and never is the transition wrought without a violent exothermy, a blast of original heat: we see it every day: the steaming sausage splits its skin: pop! and to minimize the effect, we, knowing the weakness of our institutions, have a clever way of punching holes in the meat while it cooks and before it is done. We know, I say, of Johnson's views; but we also know he was quick to discern even thick-veiled virtue and to cherish what little he found. As he fed, he conceded Anna some decent traits, certain positive capabilities, and wagered she might have in her what permits a stubborn devotion. The survey completed, he fell to inspecting his own self, for Johnson, a scientist, was interested in the truth and found it necessary not only to assemble strictly objective data, but repeatedly, it made no difference how tediously, to analyze the subject who collected it. This evening's self-examination produced the usual results: he discovered so much amiss with his own person and character that his spirit was chastened and he felt the limitations of science in his higher honesty. She might be a poor creature Adrian had chosen for him, but what was he? she might not be trustworthy, but who would soil himself with vile Johnson's destruction? The State had refused to have done with him; what could Anna hope to accomplish? Johnson, very unworthy, very mean Johnson, negligible clod, craven article, least of men, most unlovable, was manifestly neither fit to live nor fit to die, and yet Anna, lest he was in complete error, doted upon him. Blind love, oh mad sightless compulsion, nervous disorder, glandular tumult, all this hubbub over himself, how peculiar; he undertook to regard himself as if through her eyes. What did he see? But men and women are capable of the most stupendous deceptions, and when it is love that distracts, or war, then who can describe the disparity between what is and what is fancied to be there?

Now, in the midst of these lucubrations, a peculiar
situation suddenly arose: Anna had set a basket of
fruit before the Doctor: she had leaned forward in
such a way it had seemed to him not only proper but
essential to adjust his chair; his abrupt movement
may have prevented her from straightening up; noticing she still held the fruit knife firmly in her hand,
his next gesture, or inspiration, was diversionary:
he overturned the basket; she stooped, probably to
retrieve what had tumbled to the floor, tugging, for
the Doctor could not be sure what motive, at the table-
cloth and succeeding in upsetting the Doctor's glass
of wine which, thinking rapidly, he elected to attempt
to avoid, recoiling, in so doing (this was one possible
interpretation) wedging her foot, causing her to lose
her balance and to emit a cry, whether of pain, pleasure,
vengeance, frustration he had no way of knowing, nor
was he able to be certain of what prompted her to
clutch at his arm; in doubt, he failed to oppose the
sufficient amount of resistance: actually, wishing to
remain just where he was, Anna's fall, in its first phase,
established a distance between his behind and the
chair, in its second, displaced the latter and resolved
the question: they thrashed in each other's arms,
under the table, upon bruised and crushed pears and
bananas, while wine dripped onto the Doctor's nape.
Had it not been for this adventure they might never
have reached an understanding; therefore, Johnson
afterwards reflected, it was for the better they had
unburdened themselves. The Doctor did so in these
terms: "Love," he said, "is blind" (for what advantage
was there in skirting the issue?) "and despite the facts
every lover admires his mistress, though she be very
deformed of herself, yes, even if she be ill-favored,

wrinkled, pimpled, pale, red, yellow, tanned, tallow-faced, Anna, have a swollen juggler's platter face, or a thin, lean chitty face, have clouds in her face, be crooked, dry, bald, goggle-eyed, blear-eyed, or with staring eyes, she looks like a squis'd cat, hold her head still awry, heavy, dull, hollow-eyed, black or yellow about the eyes, or squint-eyed, sparrow-mouthed, Persian hook-nosed, have a sharp fox nose, a red nose, China-flat, great nose, a nose like a promontory, gubber-tushed, my good Anna," said he wiping his neck with a napkin, "rotten teeth, black, uneven brown teeth, beetle-browed, a witch's beard, her breath stink all over the room, her nose drop winter and summer, with a Bavarian poke under her chin, a sharp chin, lave-eared, with a long crane's neck, which stands awry too, her dugs like two double jugs, or else no dugs, in that other extreme, bloody-fallen fingers, she have filthy, long unpared nails, scabbed hands or wrists, a rotten carcass, she stoops, is lame, splay-footed, gouty legs, her ankles hang over her shoes, her feet stink, she breed lice, be a mere changling, a very monster, an oaf imperfect, her whole complexion savours, an harsh voice, incondite gesture, vile gait, be a vast virago, or an ugly tit, a slug, a fat fustilugs, a truss, a long lean rawbone, a skeleton, a sneaker, and to thy judgment, or mine, look like a mard in a lanthorn, whom thou, or I, couldst not fancy for a world, but hatest, loathest and wouldst have spit in her face or blow thy nose in her bosom, *remedium amoris* to another man, a dowdy, a slut, a scold, a nasty, rank, rammy, filthy beastly quean, dishonest peradventure, obscene, base, beggarly, rude, foolish, untaught, peevish Irus' daughter, Thersites' sister, Grobian's scholar; such, Anna, you are certainly not; and this little sketch, once penned by the good Reverend Burton, need only be remembered that there never arise an occasion for determining whether the likeness is just. We must cultivate the habit of looking ahead, of making constructions, of hearing the music in the score; some are able to take their rest in the lees of a royal oak still an acorn a child's bite could break. However, we will doubtless hold further conversations on the subject of our relations and prospects. Remember this, I ask no more: only unto God is it given to love and to be wise. And even so, even God. Anna, I believe you might fetch the coffee now."

Johnson was long at table. The blinds were drawn, curtains covered everything up. He ate and drank in secrecy. Illicit are the most perfect loves; speak them not, Johnson had been advised more than once, oh no, speak them not; say what you must, if something you have got to say, anything provided it not be of passion or passionately.

There are other raptures which, close, still and alone, you will discover and learn to rate very highly; but the soul that has lain in ignorance of what prayer and mystic communion may yield will neither approve nor grasp the Doctor's total submission to duck and wine, his abrupt and complete forgetfulness of the world, in which he was a stranger, and of its myriad unfed, who were as naught according to every opinion save that weak, idle, deplorable sentiment he had left, with his young manhood's impulses and all the enormities whereunto the flesh is susceptible, behind him, in jail. Masked, incognito (the Doctor fondly supposed), civility kept him company, sat in widow's weeds at his right hand, regarding his pleasure, dreaming of her own, sharing his retreat. He feasted singly at (as he visualized it) the tribe's death banquet. A toast to Henriette de Guesclin Johnson, another to Uncle Julian, one to Uncle Adrian, a fourth to Uncle Valerian, a final one to the memory of his father, Bavarian. When the ceremony was over, the homages done, he rose, lit a cigar and resumed work on his report. Mekkech eventually joined him in his study. They exchanged worried glances.

Until then, Dr Johnson had never entirely conquered the ill-feeling he bore his old friend, whose conduct, whatever its grounds, had not, he believed, been chic; and on his side, the spy had never altogether over-come the aversion, indeed the disgust excited in him by persons who were, particularly when its victims, defiled by contact with the State. But upon shaking hands, their two hearts very nearly melted; Mekkech's contempt and Johnson's pique vanished, or paled; all reserve, or virtually all, went the way of rancor; they chattered—guardedly, it is true—like boys of twelve.

Opened French doors offered a view of the dining room table littered with evidence that caught Mekkech's twinkling eye. "Samuel!" he cried, "you've had a marvelous dinner—don't deny it!" "And how I deserved it. The first in ages." "You needn't tell me." "Surely not." "I've just come from the Accuser's." "No! But of course." "He wanted to see me. Can you guess why?" "I've not the faintest idea." "Nor have I. He did see me. That was that. I felt I had to stay—at least I did stay. Good God." "Poor chap." "Do you mean me?" "You, Claude-Maxime, everyone. Your visit reminds me of so much. Had I only known. Anna provided enough for the whole city." "Well, Samuel, you know, you do look sleek." "Do I? How were things at the Palace? Are they still mistreating themselves? Has Yvette really got worms? In the factory I heard a rumor Claude-Maxime would not outlast the spring. Apparently he has. May Anna bring you some Chartreuse?"

They began again. "Samuel, you are to be envied. You think not?" "Do you think so?" "I think everyone does envy you. They're getting older, thinner, sadder, balder, but you, why, I've never seen you in better form." "It's all form, old chap," said Johnson, "that's all." They clicked their glasses. "There is not much to say. It was purely a question of the food—" "The food! Excellent!" Mekkech roared. "Appalling, rather. Yes. I was a riveter—" "A riveter! Better yet!" Mekkech roared again. "Ha! ha! exceedingly amusing," said Johnson, roaring in his turn. "We were nicely installed down there, well out of harm's way. It was, as it were, a very pure existence. The place is kept tidy and clean and while one is prevented from contaminating others, you must realize there is another side to that coin. Mekkech, dear fellow, after that sheltered life and all that hygiene, it takes some courage to come back here, where, three hours after setting foot in this apartment, I learn there is no immunity, no safety... but, on the other hand, I am afraid I have only one or two things left to learn."

"That's the effect, is it? You arrive at a fearlessness—"

"I perhaps did not make myself clear—"

"Don't tell me your first desire upon leaving prison was to return to it! Wonderful!"

"I had no desires upon leaving prison, old man, unless it was to eat, and that was not exactly a desire. At the back of my mind—" "Oh, your mind! There's not another like you in the whole country. Believe me, Samuel, believe me, not another and perhaps that is a pity, perhaps not. But, to be serious: one cannot voluptuate forever—" "That is true." "And there are things to do, matters to attend to?...."

"I don't think so. Matters attend to themselves, as you have perhaps come here to inform me. No, nothing." "Nothing?"—a hint of anger lay in the agent's voice. Oh dear, thought the Doctor, what can the trouble be? Whither are we being led? However, he repeated: "Nothing." Soberly looking his old friend, his first friend, directly in the eye, Dr John-son said once again that there was nothing, that was all he could say at the present time, and if he were wrong, he would not be so for long, the future, which he could foretell and which anyone else could foretell, would bear him out as it bore the others under, and he added, "That seems evident to me." "Yes," res-ponded Mekkech, "that's probably so." But behind those knit brows, that sincerity and excess of gravity, were they not enjoying themselves hugely? Reluctant to pass on to other subjects, so fertile and so reward-ing was this one, they retraced their steps and a second time recited their colloquy; but every good thing must have its term, such is the ardent hope of God and man. They ground at last to silence and dumbly con-templated the catastrophe. "I once spoke hastily," Johnson remarked. "I've changed my mind since then. I don't believe we'll get out. It's unthinkable. My disappointment has fallen to rags and tatters and these into dust." However, Mekkech had been neither immobilized nor a patient. Fourteen years of busy activity lay behind him. He had not been a victim, he had made victims; he hated them, hated their weakness, hated the injuries their weakness invited, the injuries to which their weakness required them to be exposed, required him to work upon them. Never had he entered a room without bringing evil tidings; a plague to others, never once had he left off insulting others; till now he was elevated to a singular ignominy, to a high level of criminal effectiveness, no more, no less, as Johnson had just finished informing him, than a weapon long use had made sick unto death of undoing and of killing, "that meanest, most common of things." Why, this black man had demanded to know, why should I soil myself with the blood of others? "Out of weakness, impudence and stupidity," Johnson had answered; "oh, to be sure, you've asked the question before: and I know how they behave: like lovesick girls they arch their backs, roll their eyes, bare their throats, and you, despairing... poor old Mekkech." The agent's envenoming stare roved and fell before his youth's companion who had somehow achieved an exemption his, Mekkech's, ferocious performances, utterly without meaning, probably without consequences, had only thrust further from his grasp. "You were born to something better than to become a champion amongst the vicious; why are you so greedy? of what are you afraid? why do you suffer?"

"Say the word, then," Mekkech murmured.

"Nothing of the sort," said the Doctor. "Matters take care of themselves." The lonely eye unblinking fixed a Mekkech of fourteen years' destruction.

"Samuel, they've turned you into a pompous bore"; it was not untrue. All the happiness and its fiction were banished. They were there to do business.

"I came to tell you you have got to be careful." "And
I received you to advise you I will be what I can and
must." "You must be on your guard, you have to
be very careful. As a matter of fact, you might be
betrayed." "Impossible, unthinkable," said the Doctor.
Mekkech grimaced; "I've reason to be quite certain
of it," he said. "I've reason to be quite certain you
have wasted your time," said Johnson, "and I am
sorry." "There are spies—you are aware of that,
aren't you?" Johnson said he was aware of nothing;
Mekkech felt as if he were alone. "I'm one, for
example. You could be sent back to prison. As
a matter of fact, that's what is going to happen."

And although they stayed together for the greater
part of the night, unwilling, each, to stir, they took
little delight or comfort in each other's presence. For
either of them, any kind of presence might have sufficed.

And so he had a few days to pass, and these he
passed glancing at his notes, thumbing through his
books, rereading old letters, making new observations
and commenting on former ones, plotting and comparing
graphs and diagrams, enjoying the fine summer weather
from his fifth-floor balcony and eating as much, as
often and as well as was humanly possible. Anna
was continually sent out in pursuit of provisions.
Because they were scarcer than ever, for there was a
dearth of everything, she was obliged to spend large
sums and at least half the day travelling through Grön
to procure the rare dainties Johnson made it plain he
had absolutely to have; she established the facts in

the course of her outings; her interlocutors, incredulous, were moved to verify her statements and representatives of the police soon joined the band of famished citizens gathered round the four garbage pails Anna carried down to the street every morning. The Doctor would now and then pause in his researches to peer down at this congress in more or less uninterrupted session; he entertained himself imagining the debates, and would now, to himself, present the case in favor, now formulate the argument against.

"Yes," Anna insisted at the precinct commissariat, "all he does is grow fat. Mainly, he eats. I'm his cook." She looked apprehensively at the soldier who was still sitting on a stool, still poring over an illustrated manual, following the dialogue with his finger. He was off duty.

"And before?"

Anna put her hand to her breast. "Before?" The soldier raised his violet eyes. "My master weighs ninety-six kilos stripped naked as a baby," she stammered. The soldier shifted his legs. "That's one thing. That's more than he weighed before. Before, he weighed less weight," she explained. "Does he ever talk about it? Oh yes, he says it was hard. He talks to me sometimes. He uses hard words. It's like singing without music, it's wonderful." Anna suddenly felt overheated. He was very patient with her, that was what he was like in his personal relations, and there wasn't anyone in the world who would say different, ah no. She scratched her scalp. Was she contented with her place? She scratched and said she thought so, but it wasn't for her to say, because she couldn't tell, she'd been there a long time but he hadn't, they'd understand what she meant. The soldier crossed his legs again and wadded his pamphlet into his hip-pocket.

"That's correct, my name's Peenie, and I want to tell you all how happy I am to be here." It was the proprietor of the building, a terrified little object, and he had only words of praise for Dr Johnson. "It's just as this lady has been telling you, a fine man and let me tell you I know a fine man when I see one and I've seen him on and off for three days. What?" cried Peenie, "is that where he's been? He has a prison record? That's a lesson for me. You can't be too careful. I can tell you it's not easy to judge at first sight and on the basis of a three days' acquaintance, and hardly what you could call an acquaintance, for you see I'm not in the habit of prying into other people's affairs, I attend to my own business and have only strictly formal contact with our tenants, they come, they go, provided the rent is paid on time I'm satisfied, and generally they pay it at the bank, not to me, so I couldn't honestly tell one from another, no, I don't think I could recognize your man, I've no memory for faces, I hope everything gets straightened out for I believe everyone deserves to get that to which he is entitled to and of course I'll bear witness, officer, believe me, I'll do anything I can to help and let me know if there's anything you want me to sign or swear to."

Anna reached out to keep from slipping further. "I buy the food and make his meals, I clean the flat." "Well," said Peenie, taking his leave, "they cart enough garbage out of that place, it probably is clean." "He likes fowl," Anna said, brimming over with resentment, "duck, pheasant, pigeons, quail, capons, grouse, anything I can get so long as it's a bird. He gets that twice a day. So I have to go out to the stores a lot for the Doctor. I come in at seven and give him his coffee. He wouldn't touch it if it wasn't me who makes it. That's all he eats for breakfast. He spends the morning getting ready. Then he eats dinner at twelve-thirty and he eats all day long and he eats another dinner at eight o'clock, all by himself, no one's there but him and me." She was panting.

The soldier made a hacking sound.

Anna was told that, from the authorities' point of view, the relation between Johnson and herself was not clear. "It's not clear?" Anna blenched. "Did he tell you that? He told me that." They were puzzled. That was all. Anna retired, sweating.

The soldier followed her into the street, caught up with her, grasped her arm. She was not surprised. He smelled fresh and of soap and water. His uniform was neat, his gun greased and slung over his shoulder, he stood quite erect, his buttocks were full and round, so was his face. Breathing deeply, the butt of his rifle thudding against her knee, he drew her to him, said: "Honey," and attempted to embrace her.

Anna was moved. "Let's go and buy something to drink," she said recklessly. "Do you drink?" "Yah Honey," he replied, not very gaily. They found an ironmonger's shop and were sold a bottle and given a corkscrew. The soldier leaned his gun against a nail-keg and drew the stopper with a swift jerk; he was robust, milk-fed, hairless, proud of his strength; he leered.

Anna decided he was serious. "You're not the drinking type," she observed, "a nice boy." He might have been eighteen, twenty-eight, thirty-eight; the important thing was that he was young and salivated

abundantly. He introduced the neck of the bottle
into his mouth and sucked, expelled air, sucked some
more. "You don't talk much, do you? You're not
the type," Anna continued. She saw his face darken;
while with bottle uplifted he swallowed noisily, his
small violet eyes, full of pleasure and pride, fixed first
the shopkeeper, then Anna, then a moving point in
the deserted street. "Do you read much?" The
soldier tendered her the bottle and puckered his face;
Anna's fondness for him increased. "Have you killed
a lot of people?" "Honey," he said, squinting through
the window, "I guess so. I've had my bayonet in
the bellies of pregnant women," he declared with
perfect candor, "and sometimes I've dug all that mess
out of their cunts and made them eat it, once I cut off
a kid's prick while his father was watching and made
the old man chew it and then I cut off the old man's
nuts, we torture them all, or they starve to death,
Honey, orders are orders, I've seen a lot, I've sure
seen a lot, I've made women drown their babies and
seen them eat them when they got hungry enough,
I've shot this little old rifle up a lot of little old assholes.
That's war, Honey, that's how it goes, I guess it's always
been that way and always will be. I'm on leave now.
I'll be going back soon."

Anna was thrilled. "Do you dream sometimes?"
she asked. He shook his head. "You know," she
went on, "sometimes I have dreams. I think of soldiers.
They're our boys and they're at war in the jungle,
and it's in the night." The soldier watched her,
expressionless. "They've put up their tents and
they've finished eating and they start drinking before
they tuck in to go to sleep. I suppose you know what
it's like, I guess you've been there." "So help me

God, Honey." "And then in this dream I'm dreaming"—she closed her eyes—"I see the dreams the
soldiers dream. They dream about home and having
a big dinner. They're all sitting around the table,
the whole family's sitting there, the mother and the
father and the brothers and the sisters and the cousins
and the aunts and the uncles, they're all telling stories,
and the mother brings in soup and celery and butter
and beer and then potatoes and walnuts and chicken
and they're glad to be there but—" The soldier
snatched up his gun, he rushed out the door to fire one
shot, two, three at a spectral pinpoint stabbing its
hilarious, erratic course towards the Place des Philosophes, in the heart of the city.

"It very much depends," said the Doctor the next
day. He stepped out upon the balcony and raised
his telescope to his eye. "It very much depends."
Ordinarily, provided visibility was good, he devoted
an hour of each morning to observations. Around
his camp-chair were disposed music stands and a high
old-fashioned copyist's desk; he had ample supplies
of paper for calculations and sketching, atlases and
astrological charts, a sextant, a protractor, dividers
and parallel rulers, and half a dozen books bound
in vellum. His schedule reserved the afternoon for
composing reports on what had transpired during
the morning watch. Drawing, reading, writing, esti-
mating—he worked slowly. Nothing seemed of greater
importance to him; while nothing could have induced
him to neglect to be thorough, or to skimp, or to appro-
ximate, his project seemed as vague, as unintentional

as it was vast, and from it he appeared to derive nothing resembling joy.

Dr Johnson's single blue eye was fitted to his telescope; a new black silk patch covered the hole where the other had been. The sky was clear. He had his telescope trained on nothing.

"Why, you're a lovely man all the same," Anna repeated. She leaned her belly against the copyist's desk.

"Prudence," the Doctor enjoined; "you're getting in over your depth again, my dear woman." He jotted down numbers on a scrap of paper. The desk teetered. "Careful there." "Oh yes you are. You know it too," she said, her voice rising. "Might you not be able to make me a sandwich?" The Doctor continued to sweep emptiness and to record figures. "Or dust the living room or somewhere else?" "You do," she persisted, "anyone can see that." He lowered his glass. "Anna, you have been drinking. You are also a lost soul. You speak from envy and spite. You have no true affection for me. Very well. I do not reproach you. Tell me about yourself." He set to adding his column of numbers.

"It's you I'm telling about," Anna insisted. "I see. What do you say to them?" "You," she spluttered inconsequently, "you never say a word, really." She knit her rust-colored eyebrows, pursed her lips. "You eat." "I do." "Is that a crime," she demanded, "to say that?" "Why, Anna, it very much depends."

The Doctor rose and guided her back to the kitchen, explaining that, "No, dear Anna, you are mistaken and certain to be deceived further; in this you are like all the rest of us: that is your fate. What are these,

after all? I beg you to look closely and critically.
Tinsel, façade, false lustre, deceit and treachery, and
so on. No, Anna, I am not what you might prefer
to think me. My habits and manners would not
stand scrutiny. I am not handsome, far from it,
I am not desirable nor lovable. Do you know, have
you heard, those young men, our heroes and our hope,
are you aware that those glorious youths regularly
use persons like myself very badly? Surely, surely
you realize it; and how right they are! Has ever
a creature existed who could rival me in offensive
traits? Who is more selfish than I? Who is more
insolent? And is not the littleness of my cruelty
fouler by many times than a gross but sincere barbar-
ity? My hair—look at me—, my hair is unkempt,
dry and unwashed, my mouth evil-smelling, my teeth
stained, my fingernails broken and yellow. I have
never once voted, I earn no money and therefore pay
no taxes, or fewer than I could if I stirred myself,
I participate scarcely at all in the life of the community,
I am not even a true enemy of the people. I am rich,
which it is not good to be, I pay my debts, but by
proving my ability to pay them it is only natural I
incur dislike. I study, and that is useless and properly suspect; unattractive, unproductive, plainly a
snob and probably worse—there you have it, I am
afraid." It soothed her. He continued: "And you,
example of sacred simplicity, upon what strange sands
you have been treading. Recollect yourself, Anna,
consider what you have done and what you must not
do again, and then go and purchase... what shall it
be? My dear Anna, I leave it to your discretion—
I am entirely in your hands." She remained posted
before the white enameled table covered with casse-

roles and pots and bird guts, scissors and feathers, a spool of white thread, chips of razor-blade and vestiges of romance.

The fine weather continued and, taking full advantage of it, Johnson went steadily on accumulating data, staring through his optic which now he pointed upwards, at the void, and now down, at his countrymen gathering in greater and greater numbers round the pails of ordures from his kitchen, edging towards the entrance of the building and loitering, so Anna said, in the hallway. He sent Anna out after a newspaper. It was a pretext; when she returned from her errand, he asked what had detained her. She complained of having had trouble getting past the crowd on the stairway; he accepted her explanation without comment and retired to the balcony where, settling down to read the news, he gestured deferentially, amicably to those persons who, anxious expressions on their faces, were watching his movements from windows of buildings across the street.

The day's informations included an account of wild fluctuations in corn; he learned as well that the bottom was fairly falling out of pig-bristles, cochineal and glue; that a little boy had just invented a powerful bomb; that the obol had sunk another twenty-seven points at Brussels, thirty at Geneva; further disquieting statistics from the United States: the American male's average height had attained six feet one inch, his length eleven centimeters, and what would be the effect upon national manners of the use of Rubbabub by the ideal example of American womanhood? In another sector of the world an élite division had undergone a calvary: it had been lost, it had been found, it had been praised and held up to scorn, it had been sacrificed, written off and written on, then ambushed, subsequently annihilated, but disengaged and finally decorated, it was coming home, it was going back into action. Locally, two hundred thousand copies of the Objector's recent attack upon the Accuser had been printed by the government: sales of this pamphlet had been disappointing; whereupon the Bureau of Censorship had pronounced its interdiction, confiscated and destroyed the entire impression; this measure had necessitated the free distribution of three hundred thousand copies; and an order had been signed calling for the arrest of anyone in whose possession the banned treatise could be found. In addition, tales of ships sunk, nine murders had occurred since Tuesday last, the hog cholera epidemic was abating, the birthrate was increasing, a detail sufficient in itself to buck up your glum pessimists. The Doctor put the journal aside and turned to his more serious occupations which, several hours later, a knock on the door obliged him to suspend.

It was Puddick he admitted. Having introduced himself and having presented specimens of his work Johnson took care not to touch, the novelist, affecting the air of a damned fine fellow, swore he had had a regularly filthy time of it getting through all those blokes and remarked that, despite his torn coat and missing collar, it was bloody well worth it, oh by God, and that it was high time they made one another's acquaintance. The Doctor's name was on everyone's lips, said he, the town was talking about no one else, the Doctor had become profoundly topical, profoundly typical, some were maintaining; he, Puddick, had a nose for essences, that was his game, and what did he, Johnson, think of that? Puddick had a hunch he,

Johnson, would think a great deal, at least—even preferably—something of that, perhaps a small but pithy amount a few sentences might be able to convey, eh? He had come with writing materials as well as written materials and he hoped he had not disturbed Johnson's meditations and work, curiosity concerning the exact nature of which, Puddick confessed, had, ak, been his motive for intruding. They were both intellectuals, he went on, men of sensibility and conscience, what was more, having analogous concerns and contiguous interests, they were, so he judged, of the same cut, bred in the same zone, under one vast heaven, and alone, yes, companions and sharers of the same spirit, quand même, quand même. And what could be more reasonable, he cried, what more just than for him to have inclined before all the laws of attraction and to have come humbly and hopefully to call? For, he concluded, we are all, each one of us, engaged in a quest...

Needless to say, whether or not Johnson could make head or tail of this preface, begun with a fraternal warcry and ended in a humid blubbering, he gave out no hint of having understood a syllable of it. Perspiring after his hard climb and hard fight, exalted by sentiments whose utterance seemed to open up a very fair prospect but depressed by the Doctor's failure or refusal to respond as one brother to another, young Puddick floundered directly, perhaps accidentally, who can tell? to the heart of the matter, demanding:

"Where, my good man, do you think you are going?" And then: "What do you think of your chances of making it?"

Johnson blinked. He suggested they might be more comfortable in his study. "And you," he asked, "do you really think it was wise to have come here?"

Puddick was assembling the elements of a reply when it struck him as highly paradoxical that he, an individual to whom by virtue of an unique talent and station the care of the language had been confided, could never hold what he qualified as an important conversation without experiencing that sensation of dreadful unsupport from which a man afraid of height will suffer when halfway up a ladder. Invariably, Puddick realized, what was begun as a civil exchange would get out of hand: would transform itself into a desperate scrambling and clutching and shinnying back to solitude and muteness. Every effort to communicate on an elevated plane led straight to nausea. He could articulate nothing but his humiliation. Why, thought he, this is frightful! Then he said: "I have always defended you, after a fashion of speaking."

"Have you?" Johnson replied, deciding to give back blow for blow. "The essential merits of the feeble are embellished, indeed may be said to be created by their sufferings. Accuse Johnson? defend Johnson? Pure irrelevance. It is not innocence cries scandal aloud."

"But," Puddick insisted, groping for the thread, "you don't even bother to defend yourself. One would think that, normally, a person who had been treated the way you have—"

"Once upon a time, a person treated as I have been treated would have resented it. Would have reacted against it; an eye for an eye was the code governing a normal man's response to ill-treatment. Well, we are done with all that. With such men, such codes, such injuries. Once upon a time..."

And the Doctor pronounced a very pretty, but a

very long, harangue full of glittering antitheses, sonorous phrases, trenchant examples, rich images and noble periods which have got to be omitted in a summary. He dealt first with the present outlook, next with his own; he spoke of gods, dominations, and of powers; then of government and of subordination; of subjects and of authority; of divers little tensions and conflicts; of plot; of style. He expressed his opinions on the geometry of human relationships. He described the limitations of art. He expertly re-enacted the battle of the books. And he did all this in less than two hours.

"Well, well," said he, very pleased with himself, "you have a keen intellect, haven't you? Yes, a rare sensibility, a fund of talent, you have them all, just as you say. But I believe my housekeeper has arrived; will you stay for dinner? Eh? Don't stand there cringing. Haven't you a tongue in your head? Speak up, little man, speak up. What's that? Caution, duty, obedience, modesty? Ah, I think I understand, please don't make apologies, you are expected elsewhere, is that it? Or you have a chapter to write, or a play to criticize, or a phrase to polish. I must then bid you good evening. Anna," the Doctor called, "you will show this young gentleman to the door," and Johnson went to the bathroom to rinse his hands.

Before beginning the descent, Puddick's ten stubby fingers had groped for and not succeeded in locating the button that operated the light; his search had led him to step on a foot; "Excuse it, please," he whispered; then he touched his palm to a nose and moist stirring lips. "Pardon me," he said, moving away and pressing his face against an unknown neck; a gust of warm breath washed his cheek and ear when his elbow contacted a belly. "I am so sorry," and he rubbed his genitals upon a masculine hip, his calf against a naked leg. But by now his eyes had become accustomed to the dark; many hands were reaching out, not to deter, nor to speed, but to soothe him; the softest gradations of black and grey indicated the direction he was to take, gentle, anonymous nudges and tugs drew him to the steps and he slowly made his in a certain sense pontifical way down between two files of human beings: "Thank you... thank you... thank you": he exhaled the words like a benediction, the obscurity yielded to a dusty red, he reached the entrance as others before him had reached the throne or the stone and in the street it was a summer's early evening, the sweet odor of rotting waste and the smell of men. He wondered what to do. What now? he asked himself. It had been a mistake to go. It had overexcited him. It had stupified him. He had gone where he had no right to enter. He had seen what he had no right to see, heard what he had no right to hear. To be that close to a man and yet so far away... had it not been for the intense blue flame of creativity, the terrible imperative to give expression to a swarm of sentiments and conceptions, to the richness and diversity of what his irreplaceable self contained, had it not been for all this, all he had to offer the world, he might then and there, oh a thousand muses bear witness and tremble! have abjured his vocation, yes, broken his quill and deeper than did ever plummet sound, drowned his inkpot... He pondered the advisability of emigrating, he would steal across the frontier, he would deceive the customs officials, he would travel light, a tooth-brush, a safety

razor, a bar of soap, then he would make a new beginning, he would rewrite his novels, alter the names of
places and characters, change his own name. But
perhaps, to do it properly, he ought to re-enlist in the
army whence all inspiration comes, where one suffers
and causes others to suffer, collects material and revi-
talizes one's yen to speak. Or perhaps a more certain
means to this end would be to plunge himself into
a Trappist community; however, the sweet peace
of the monastery seemed to sort ill with his fiery temper
and love of action: he would not retire: he would offer
his services to the rebels, he would deliberately choose
a losing side, if one might be found, and by intimate
involvement in the fate of man either watch the creative
flame flicker and die, or burn with redoubled violence
in exile, in thick strife, danger and defeat. But for
the time being... he had an hour before the scheduled
supper with Yvette and the Accuser. He would not
go; was he a slave, a lackey, a creature? or a master
of the great themes of modern thought and the most
significant patterns of contemporary feeling, a writer
and a creator? Then where would he go? He had
a wide choice of alternatives, for he had been provided
with a library, a writing room, a thinking room, a
small room for gymnastics in which to keep fit, a
consultation chamber and an administrative office,
which was a dark, gritty, draughty room he used when
he felt the need of summing up, taking stock, facing
himself honestly, reasoning maturely or when there
was a technical difficulty to overcome or a barren
period to emerge from; or when, prostrated with awe
before the grandeur of his intentions and cast down
into a very slough of despond by the meagerness of
the resources at his command, he wanted the ordinary

man's comforts and petty certitudes. The administrative office, for which he now seemed to have a preference, was a kind of museum, or warehouse, stuffed with just what Puddick had to have within reach when it occurred to him that, for instance, every book he sent to the printer meant the deforestation of half a province. Ranged against the walls were japanned cabinet files with labeled drawers containing ticketed classifiers; above the files, mounting to the ceiling, were shelves, framed diplomas and certificates; he had envelopes, folders, agendas, ledgers, blank, lined, and quadrilled notebooks and noteblocks, stitched, gummed, wirebound and looseleaf, strongboxes padlocked and combinationlocked, keyrings with springs, without springs but with clasps and catches, paper and cellulose and adhesive tape, wrapping paper, note paper in every format, foolscap, onionskin, doublestrong, eggshell, glossy, raisin and double Jesus, cardboard, typewriters, large and small, some so large it took two men to lift one of them, some so small they could fit into one's vest-pocket, with various keyboards, pica type, italics, typewriter ribbons violet, green, blue and bi-colored, adding machines, directories, telephones, dictaphones, pencils and pens and a supply of penpoints and erasers and blotters pink and white, fresh and used, postage stamps, mint and cancelled, scales, letteropeners, sponges, rubber stamps, he lacked nothing, not even a glass paperweight which, when the situation or his mood called for it, and it was often called for and loudly, he would pick up, hug to his breast, shower kisses upon, say sweet things to, look fondly at and shake, at first gently, then with force, finally with violence, so as to cause the snow to fall upon Hansel and Gretel imprisoned within,

178

and while he agitated the paperweight, he would
speak to the children, at the outset softly, next in a
severe voice, at last in a shout. What a pleasure,
after breakfast or before his exercizes, or after his devo-
tionals, or before taking a decision or after taking off
his hat, or coat, or in warm weather his shirt, his
shoes, his trousers, to address his little friends, good
God yes! to stir, to rattle, to thump, to coo, to scold,
to bellow and curse: "My precious, my dear ones,
my rascals, scoundrels, little bitch! little swine! whore!
bugger!" dear God, to bury them under a tiny blizzard
of snow flying thicker, faster, deeper. Yes indeed, what
a pleasure, thought he as he passed through the Square
of St Hippolyte-the-Unresourceful, crossed the Aegillian Bridge—he discovered he had lost his bearings,
either by mischance or good fortune. It was a sign:
he organized his critical faculties to interpret it: he
was either taking the most indirect route possible to
pleasure, in which case this devious, reluctant approach,
this veritable retreat, cast automatic doubt upon his
true and secret attitude towards the object; or he was,
unconsciously, subconsciously, obeying a mysterious
voice and effectively moving away from pleasure, pro-
ceeding elsewhere, down the Via Nemausa, towards
the Arch of Disaster that framed the Obelisk of Despair.
Ha! he muttered, there is then something in me that
rises up against the common consolations, will have
none of the facile response, the begging of a question.
Good God, yes, I'll take no pap, I'm not made to
parrot party lines and platitudes, piss when the
leader drinks, no, as an artist I'm a freely enterprising
spirit, I'll piss, puke on my own, a captive I cannot be,
my beak's not to be teazeled with the nozzles of boat-
swains' pipes, what, I? who, Puddick? Ho ho! not I,

I haunt the tempest, I laugh at the Archer, I shed my own sicknesses. Clocktowers began to peal the hour; he put on an expression of proud, dauntless independence, squeezed his buttocks together, drew a deep breath and, exclaiming what a lover of freedom was he, flung bravely to the right and bolted into the courtyard of the Accuser's Palace.

As might be expected, Samuel Johnson scribbled and drew and counted and puttered about and drove his poor housekeeper to drink and intriguing with young soldiers right up to the last minute. He had spent the morning with his neck craned over the balcony railing, for nothing but the announcement of a meal could induce him to quit his chair, and this being low, and the railing high, it was awkward to obtain and onerous to keep an unimpeded view of the street. Dead set against peering through, he would never have managed to peer over the bars had it not been for his long torso, and a pillow. He would gaze down for a quarter of an hour, chewing his lip, then he would look at the notebook on his knees, write a sentence or a phrase, look up, elevate his chin, flash a grin at his audience before resting his chin on the iron, then hump, hitch, shuffle and wriggle until his cheek covered the spot his chin had occupied a moment before, and thus, his head parallel to the rail, his one eye would be in a fairly good, at least under the circumstances the best possible, position to observe the scene below; a little later, back to the description he was composing; after this, back to the phenomena he was describing. They were few and minor. Nevertheless, he had written these words at the top of the page: "It shall go on and on, forever on and on"; beneath this, a space; under which, in a hand revealing virtually nothing beyond a certain pessimism, with rounded vertically slanted characters and lines falling to the right: "...the street washed over by a running tide of shadow... the minute, the various creatures lazing and swaying in the tepid shallows... life whose substance itself is an airy vision, a film, containing something dense, something brilliant... a paroxysm of mirth... which like an abrupt disturbance in a secluded, stagnant pool, far from the sift and slide of Ocean, in a backwater... the to and fro motion of barely stirring silt... it is hard to believe in the last agony and decay of things, in anything but this nothing and the perfect, gratuitous autonomy of metaphors..."

The doorbell rang as Johnson was screwing and swiveling up and over for another peep at the banality, the sight of which, evidently, could move him to write balderdash and, as we know, speak bonnyclabber. The doorbell was still ringing when, twenty minutes later, the Doctor made another entry in his notebook. "Anna," he said. He had a fresh idea and put it down too. "Anna. Woman. Maid. Good attentive Anna. Oh, are you there, Anna? Anna, where the Devil are you? I'm not coming, Anna, it shan't avail you, don't be timid, woman, go see who's at the door. Anna, I have not an unmarred opinion of you as it is, answer that blasted door. What's happened to her? Is this desertion? Anna!"

He rose. This time there were two men on the landing. Behind them were a dozen, fifteen, twenty other persons, by-standers. The two men were large. They were crouching down, their lightweight blue pinstripe stretched tight over shoulders, backs, rumps, hatbrims and roasts for faces thrust against the door-frame; one was picking at the button with his thumb-nail, the other said it was stuck, the first squinted up at the Doctor, who said: "Never mind. Will you come in and investigate in the light?" He retired before them. The note thrilled through his several rooms while the two men stood rocking on their heels, heads covered, double-breasted, exchanging winks, and blushing. "Very interesting," said one of them. "Very interesting," said his colleague. They went into Johnson's study. One of them stood upon the patch where the oriental carpet was most worn; he pumped up and down and wrung his enormous hands. "Would you care to sit down?" "No thanks." Johnson turned to the other who was combing his hair. "And you?" "No thanks." They surveyed the furniture about which there was nothing remarkable save perhaps for the several hundred stuffed birds enshrined in windowed cabinets and under glass hemispheres. One of the two, to facilitate his determinations, drew out a notebook and pencil; the Doctor was convinced this was a bluff. What was his surprise when indeed the policeman proved he knew how to write "You do your own stuffing?" Johnson was asked. "No," he replied promptly; "a taxidermist attends to that." "What about this iron bird?" "That is a bronze bird." "What about it?" "Why," said the Doctor, "I don't know. Do you admire it?" "Where did you get it?" "It was the gift of the man who made it, a sculptor," and Johnson mentioned the sculptor's name. "Do you recognize his work?" "He sounds like a foreigner. When did you see him last? What are your relations with him? Where does he live?" "He is no longer alive." "No longer alive. Dead, you mean?" "Dead. Why do you ask me these questions?" "We're plain-clothesmen." Dr Johnson smiled. "You're dressed very nicely, both of you. Tell me—" he began. "No, you tell us," they chorused. "Well." "Any of these birds rare birds?"

The Doctor put on his jacket and, having himself attempted and failed to stop the ringing, picked up the telephone and asked to speak to the building super-intendent; he felt a hand on his elbow; he replaced the receiver. They were in a hurry. "Peenie should look into this, notwithstanding, for he has his duty to perform also." "Jesus, Faloney," cried one of the inspectors, "ever seen so many birds?" Faloney edged towards a pair of Carpathian falcons, stared at their savage glass eyes and distended talons; he should have liked to have been invited to slide back the parti-tion and to touch them, to stroke the feathers, the Doctor thought; of a sudden he wondered what had become of Anna. "All dead. Guess they'd make a mess if they were alive, wouldn't they. Live here all by yourself?" Faloney asked. "Yes," said Johnson, "bar-ring my housekeeper who is probably being tupped by an infantryman at this very instant. No, on the other hand," the Doctor corrected himself, "that is not likely." "Is that so? Nice place you have, except for that bell—" "About whose ringing, I submit, we might—for there are three of us here to tackle the problem, and we are all grown men—be able to do something." "Pay a lot of rent?" "Every tri-mester." "Mind if I ask you how much?" "Not at all." "My sister-in-law could use a place like this," Faloney observed.

The Doctor secured the balcony doors, straightened

some papers on his desk and offered his arm to the nearer of the two men. The plainclothesmen blew blasts on their whistles, the Doctor broke wind, then they, the three of them, all grown men, walked out and down the stairs. Johnson was looking very well that morning. He had on shined shoes and a new patch. He spoke to everyone he passed, if only to say good day or I trust you are in good health; no one responded to these greetings, but this was not significant, nor was it unusual, the Doctor continued to offer them, feeling it was expected of him and believing they were grateful for a word or two, and of course they were.

Thus pinioned, bathed in much uncritical attention, counting his blessings, Dr Johnson reached the ground floor. He turned first to one guide, then to the other, speaking in an undertone and lifting his eyebrows. He felt their arms tighten quickly, reassuringly about his, their shoulders press closer, and Faloney licked his lips and said to his comrade, "All set, Maloney," and Maloney scooped some wax from his ear and looked abashedly at the end of his snub nose, and Johnson practiced his rapid grin, and Faloney adjusted his jockey shorts which had been threatening to ride up, and Faloney's comrade Maloney scratched his honest Celtic testicles and patted his fly, and then they were ready to go and for come what might. The door swung wide; the abrupt out-of-doors blaze smote them; wincing, they clung to each other and then, as an integral unit, in step, intimately, they walked forth, they advanced down the street lined with spectators while the doorbell cried beneath the roof and whistles shrilled through the unbelievable quiet. And the tolerant world, the marvelous world, multiple bits of colored glass leaded into doorways and shopfronts and hung

in windows, the world of griped paste gems infinite to
see, caught rays of passionate sunlight and flung them
upon the trio regarded, in all its splendor and variety,
by indifference. It was simply more than Johnson,
an intelligent man whatever his faults, could compre-
hend. When a pregnant skyliner long overdue slash-
ed against a tall building and spat its issue over the
naked grey walls, tired them in bright red roe, and as
a rain of fiery rubbish and bloody tears, flakes of burning correspondence and spheres of flaming petrol cas-
caded down from above, with a peculiar gasp, Johnson had the impression it was not new, no, nor exceptional, the most ancient precedents and the most ele-
mentary desires sanctioned these institutions, and he
was right. As though from nowhere a human being
materialized and proceeded to volatilize: a living torch
it was, expensively and tastefully dressed; one mass
of fire, it sped meteorlike at right angles to their line
of march, curved, ran round them once or twice and,
its brief hour of vainglory spent, shot into an impasse
to die. A moment later, this identical scene was
repeated by, this time, a woman, whose body was
afire from the waist down and whose touching face,
pathetic grimaces and gestures drew expressions of
sympathy from her fellow citizens, and howls from
dogs. Johnson and the policemen marched on to
judgment and justice, feeling greatly out of place
and as if in the way, although in truth they were just
where they belonged. But the idea of awkwardness
prevailed, and made them trip, stub their toes and
cling to each other more firmly than before; they
gave and received a measure of comfort; they marched on, arms entwined like three graces in an enchanted garden, through this enormous manifestation,

amidst colorful entrails which, pinwheeling stiffly in midair and writhing like serpents on the tar, appeared to the Doctor to glow with a certain elemental heat, to palpitate with a kind of lust, at any rate to shriek their need of the augurer. A tear of delight trembled at the corner of his eye. And now the most authentic screams claimed his consideration. Soldiers rushed by, dragging equipment or culprits, bullets sprang and rebounded, pistols were out, trenchknives unlimbered, the looters were cut down and finished off with steel. No one relished having to act his part. There was the peace to disrupt and the peace to restore. Everyone was doing his level best, that was plain, and hang the cost, as they say. What more can one ask? What more can one say? One must be reasonable. One must accept people for what they are. Man is perfectable; but a long road remains to be traversed and a great distance will be overcome by patient, unremitting effort, by labor, by sacrifice, by dedication, by many things, but not by leaping hastily to rash conclusions. Johnson must have realized this; from relief, from pride, from satisfaction, he quivered, his shoulders festooned and his clothing daubed with the work of Providence. They three strode dutifully on withal; there were forty-four passengers dead, and dead were the pilot, a man of great moral rectitude, a co-pilot who commanded a salary almost as high, and an engaging young stewardess, a bachelor or arts whose initials were D.I. and whose left hand, perfectly intact, softly veined, milky white, lay there at his feet. Yielding to Johnson's earnest and pious solicitations, one of his escorts retrieved that pretty hand, and thus prevented it from becoming spoiled, or consumed, or lost, or put to inappropriate use; it was little

enough, indeed, Johnson could not have done less.
Well now! Here they were at the river. And
over there, yonder, on the northern bank was the
Cathedral, to the left, the Faculty of Medicine was
behind it; directly before them, on the far side of the
Place des Philosophes presently filled with a host of
restive people who seemed to be hiding something,
was the Palace of Justice; to the right of it, the Accuser's
Palace; and behind that imposing structure, the ter-
minus. And now they were on the bridge of Peter
the Spastic, crossing to the other side, leaving the side
Johnson preferred, going to the one he did not prefer.
How unfortunate that a river must have two sides,
like a coin, like a man, that where you find one side you
have only to look and you will discover a second and
the second one once found the thing to do is to choose,
which is the regrettable aspect of it all, not because
choosing brings on the troubles or errors it does at
least half the time bring on, but which might be brought
on without choosing, but because it is usually a fraud,
the whole thing. The Doctor felt himself in strong
agreement with that man they had beheaded in the
preceding winter and whose last words, when given the
opportunity to pronounce them, if he had any, or die
in silence, had been that to the best of his knowledge
he had never in all his life been presented with a gen-
uine option. He had hummed and hawed and screwed up his face and scratched his head and lost it. But
enough of that. They were over the bridge, across
the river and upon the great square. Further progress was blocked by that vast herd of enthusiasts.
Loudspeakers mounted on portable aluminum towers
were giving out information, but the equipment was
faulty or incorrectly adjusted or tuned and what were,

presumably, lucid statements, emerged as a succession of roving burbles and plopping sounds interspersed with twitters; for the greater part, the people stood with their heads thrown back, their eyes open or shut, awaiting an enactment. Orcus, Leader of the Games, was doubtless circulating through the crowd with his deputies. "...misplaced pistons, faulty cables, broken windshield-wipers and sabotage," Johnson heard amidst a storm of static and effects. Language of this order was capable of provoking omaphagistic bacchanals. A small airplane crashed in a nearby street. Women began to emit strange, subdued cries, blotches of color appeared on men's throats and cheeks. "...dilute gasoline, powdered emery in the machinery, blurred charts, broken parts; inexperienced ground crews, conked-out engines, the big chop, corruption in high places, sorrow below..." These experiments in free living ordinarily last until twilight; then the celebrants are whipped off the Place des Philosophes after having consumed every trace of aerial tragedy, cached bits of steel, copper tubing, rubber fittings, glass and wire in pockets, in shoes, in handbags and satchels and battened their ration of meat and mohair seat-coverings... after having cleaned up, licked the platter clean, bones, skin, guts, tucked it all away. Thus history is made, *ma lolotte*, by men. A cycle of eating, assimilating, ejecting, staggering expenditures and renewals, reconstitutions and dismemberments: production, consumption, production, consumption. And man is instrumental to all that: it could be managed without him, his intervention has added nothing; but he's here, here he may very possibly remain, and while he's about, that's his purpose, that's what you'll see him do, and nothing else.

Everything's in serene equilibrium, *mon ange*, we have a perfect stability, a restfulness guaranteed by logic and nature: matter enters different forms and orifices and departs them by the vents the great architect has supplied, there are permutations, there are combinations, but the forms endure, so does the substance, the Lord giveth and the Lord taketh away, but only apparently and not for long; there is naught real, naught apprehensible, naught meaningful but this movement, this *rerum concordia discors*, but this naught, but the eternal transition, the eternal recurrence of things; time...

Ah, time... all through the night, the dead white windows of aircraft factories lining the river paint pale faith in the water, which, laden with the nation's excrements, winds its way to the sea.

There was no going that way; so they went another, circling the edge of the crowd, picking their way through obscure streets, at last reaching a point fifty yards from the Palace of Justice. The plainclothesmen blew their whistles. A group of guardsmen charged, a corridor was chopped clear and the Doctor was piloted through. Once within a large room, he found himself alone, unattended and neglected, adrift in a press of important persons. For ten minutes, for ten more they dissented and concurred, shouting, struggling, their eyes bulging, their chalky faces distorted by feeling, waving their skinny fists, their old infirm bodies trembling. They were advocates, judges, legislators, magistrates.

"No," said one, "no, you'll never convince me. Justice—"

"But I agree," insisted a second, "no one has a greater contempt for Justice than I—"

"However, you do not seem to accord Grace the value I would—"

"I too would destroy, crush—"

"One must burn, slaughter—"

"Kill and maim," broke in a third.

"Quite," squealed a fourth, "kill and maim the enemy, no quarter—"

"None," hissed a fifth; "with fire and sword—" "All of them, men, women—" "The aged and the infantile, the whole and the decrepit; for what difference does it make?"

"It makes none; why not?"

"Why not? Once you've begun—"

"Why put a stop to it? Why are we on earth? What else have we to do? Misery, woe—"

"That's it, misery and woe."

"Woe and misery..."

By and large, they spoke well, well enough, with ample fervor and care, their arguments were not merely convincing but irresistible, and Johnson was well on his way to becoming persuaded when Porn, yes, Porn, jovial, cherubic, and still alive, came in by a side door. The clerk raised his voice. The speedy trial was to begin. "Let him come forward."

However, the Objector was there, yes, the Objector, Lechecul himself: "Just one moment," said he, "not so fast." "You are out of order." "That is as it may be," he replied, brandishing a text; 'A heretic,' Bossuet writes, 'is a man with an opinion'; the roots of opinion lie in choice. Well, what could be more absurd than

to maintain that this man, of all men, has ever manifested—" "Do you follow? Do you follow?" cried
a voice in Johnson's ear. "My specialty is corpor-
ative law, but the regulations are unambiguous.
They hold, man, they hold," bellowed Johnson's
informant. "What the Devil could a counselor do for
you in such a situation? Well, put case he might be of
psychological help to you—but to admit your need
of psychological support would be to diminish your
stature to such a point as to make a bloody joke of this
trial, heh heh. No, they've made the required provisions. Listen to me. 'In his pleading he'—who?
the lawyer who is capable of the imprudence of defending a heretic—, 'he should conduct himself properly in three respects. First, his behaviour must be
modest and free from prolixity or pretentious oratory.
Secondly, he must abide by the truth, not bring forward any fallacious arguments or reasoning, or calling
false witnesses, or introducing legal quirks or quibbles
if he be a skilled lawyer, or bring counter-accusations'
—I advise you to pay strict attention." "I am," said
Johnson. "I continue: 'especially in cases of this
sort, which must be conducted as simply and sum-
marily as possible.' Do you see it now? Allow me
to complete the picture. 'Thirdly, his fee must be
regulated'—well the fee is of no consequence here.
Granted such a man could be found in this
city—"

"You're quite right," Johnson interrupted, "we can
dispense with lawyers." "Can you? Not unless you
first give up the notion of a defense... and even then,
ah, who knows? The next point is crucial: 'Nevertheless, if he unduly defends a person already suspect
of heresy, he makes himself as it were a patron of that

heresy.' My good man, your position could not, perhaps, be worse."

Matters advanced. The Doctor advanced several paces. Porn placed his right hand upon Johnson's head. "I conjure you," he intoned, "by the bitter tears shed on the Cross by our Saviour the Lord Jesus Christ for the salvation of the world, and by the burning tears poured in the evening hour over His Wounds by the most Glorious Virgin Mary, His Mother, and by all the tears shed in this world by the Saints and the Elect of God, from whose eyes He has now wiped away all tears, that if you be innocent you do now shed tears, but if you be guilty that you shall by no means do so."

"What a farce," grumbled the Objector. Johnson began to laugh. One tear trickled down one cheek, emanating from his one eye.

"And now what are you going to do?" the Objector demanded, assembling his notes and wadding them into his briefcase; without waiting for a reply, he stamped out of the courtroom.

Part the Fourth:

IGNORANTIO ELENCHI

Another fourteen years. This term must have been just as unpleasant as the first, and were there to be a third, it would doubtless be more trying than the second. Johnson had no luck at all. But no, it was not simply a question of luck. Surely not; had one the time, the vigor, it could be satisfactorily explained, were that necessary, or desirable, or worth the effort. You have simply no idea what it costs in effort to provide no more than an unsatisfactory explanation of anything, and the thought of writing out the scene in which, after an amazing series of exploits, Puddick met a hero's end, or of following Porn to the ignominious end of his dazzling career, or of tracing Anna's downfall, or of rendering a fuller account of what precipitated Mekkech's self-destruction, or of telling the heart-rending story of Julian's death and the dissipation of the Johnson billions, the very thought, I say, of undertaking these immense and uniformly somber labors, all of which, even were they to be accomplished, would contribute precious little to clarifying the Johnson Problem, only confirms my desire to put an end to my apology. That I began it at all, for I knew whither it would have to take to me, is even more astonishing than my having been able to grub along this far. But one thing leads fatally to another. For example:

Over a period of forty years during which our people has lived and died as never it did before, to the hilt and for a purpose, we have gradually developed and as if it were the very rock of salvation clung to the belief that our sort and kind are unique, that we have been chosen, have been distinguished from other nations. Any account of the new Grön must begin with remarks upon this sentiment of exclusiveness which has unified us. This is no joke: we have a common mission, we are a serious people. If we have undergone hardships while waging the good fight, our moment's distress has been soothed, our midnight doubts have been relieved by the notion they—struggle, anguish, our mortal concern—are incomprehensible to others and we ourselves out of all touch with all other zones.

Our neighbors have respected our desire for privacy, for isolation. No one has troubled to pierce or try the cordon sanitaire wherewith we have girt our territories. Never have we, during these past forty years, been menaced by invasion; the reports foreign diplomats send back to their capitals are as strong a guarantee against trouble as would be an army ten times as large as the one we have now, and the one we have now has no equal in Europe. Oh, to be sure, trade does yet go on, on a negligible scale: nothing of the very little we produce seems to appeal to the international market and this, you may be certain, is no accident: our manufacture is rigorously supervised, we have limited our exports, levied prohibitive duties and when necessary added insult to malpractice in order to discourage foreign traders. Commercial exchanges continue chiefly because of the habit merchants have of buying and selling, because they prefer to be in any kind of business rather than completely out of it: well, indecent traditions constitute a challenge to virtue, virtue thrives when exercized in adversity. Journalists come here from abroad and usually leave, or are expelled. The international trains run, once or twice a month, and nine-tenths empty; the airlines do a crashing fine business; our main port, St Luc, is as active as ever, for we are prosecuting the war with unabating determination. We still do receive a few tourists who at summer's end return home, saying they were unable to believe their eyes; sociologists used to pay us visits, today it's ethnologists, tomorrow it will be archaeologists; but that afflictive swarm of prurient, insolent students attracted to every continental dung-heap or ossuary has been kept away from Grön. In a word, if we maintain relations with the outside world, those relations are formal and have the one valuable effect of constantly reminding us of what we are.

We are, we believe, totally unlike anyone else. Fortunately, we have nothing to say to anyone else, surely nothing to learn from anyone else; fortunately, because we no longer have the means to say anything to anyone not of our company, no Aimée, not you, not I: there is no longer any possibility of misunderstanding, of being betrayed by explanations, there is no longer any language barrier, none of those appalling dialogues, those apings, lip-readings, those weird and pointless debates, unnatural exchanges, absurd get-togethers. The age of communication is, thank God for it, over for us. We are what our silence represents us to be. There is no proclaiming that. We want nothing with disciples.

That is the revolution. What a revolution! Think of it: no one rebelled, no one revolted, and not only was plenty of blood shed when the thing began, almost as much is still being shed forty years later.

These four decades of the Accuser's sovereignty

ended today with his death, by asphyxiation. Here
are the salient particulars. Other treatments having
failed to secure happy results, Claude-Maxime hit
upon the expedient Louis XV is thought to have
employed with a degree of success. He directed
Grimoald to have the police clean up, mop up the
city, to repair the deplorable condition of things, to
take advantage of the excessive number of those things,
between tea-time and the cocktail hour to round up
a minimum *yield* of thirty strays, whores, vagrants,
beggar children; in short, simultaneously to purge
Grön of unsightly excrescences and to supply him with
what he needed for a daily bath of blood which, he
fancied (the Objector fancied the exact contrary;
no medical authority was consulted; the question
will bear further examination), would reinvigorate
and stimulate him, make him new, young, bold again.
The Objector is known to have considered such remedies extreme. As so often proves true, he was both
right and wrong: they were not remedies at all, and
by contenting himself with a less generous yield,
Claude-Maxime might have avoided drowning. But
who can tell? He was an elderly man and loved to
bathe. His fierce modesty deprived him of a bathing
attendant. This morning, upon getting into, or upon
getting out of, we may never know which, upon entering or leaving his warm tub, it would appear that,
having posed his foot upon a chenille bathmat, he, or
his foot, slipped; he fell.

And now... as an official historian it is my duty, is
it not, situated as I am, with the information I have
at my fingertips, with those few gifts you will perhaps
allow are mine and which ought to suffice for the
task, it is my solemn obligation to sum up, wouldn't

you say? If not my duty, then whose? It is evening now. We are in national mourning. The streets are deserted. The canals have been skimmed and dredged. A curfew has been declared. I am alone, in my little house, up here in my study, in a delicate position. Twenty-four years ago it occurred to Claude-Maxime a register should be kept; for nineteen years it has been my task to collect and catalogue documents, supervise the writing of the annals; today, the Prince is dead. Where Lucius should answer, speak loud dithyrambs, he only whispers in a broken meter. Should not the winds be freighted with the tale? should not the globe's four corners be advised of the event and our heavy sorrow? There is a shadow over earth; deceased is that star of excellent light, the sun is out. What has been done before and in other places upon such occasions I know only too well, I know how they have made great moan; but my fingers are numb, I am reduced to making a small noise, this is a personal communication—no, it is not even that. We are, you, Aimée, at a pleasant fifty-three crying you have had enough, I at forty-eight murmuring, who have scarce begun, we are initiates, as it were: we do not speak to each other, for look you and see, to speak is to betray. It is my land and people I refuse to wrong; they I love indeed, I love them only, this depleted soil, this quiet society of subdued men. I'll not leave.

If anything in what I have written here strikes you as peculiar or astonishing, it is surely not because of what some tongues less mutinous than cavilling, of what some minds less critical than confused have called, and doubtless in all good faith thought to be, our disorder, but rather because they, whom I do not deign to chide, and you, whom I would do my best to comfort, have either fallen far behind the emergent reality and have ceased entirely to glimpse our times' meaning, or have, for whatever be the reason, sought to divorce themselves from a society of which the military situation is the soul and atmosphere. It cannot be done. We are all in one boat, my dear friend, and are gone far out to sea. Do you propose to swim for it? For what? For distant shores, far out of sight. Others have gone that way? So they have: watching them thrash through the water, we have seen them disappear—over the horizon? or beneath a wave? Having sought to evade the duties stipulated in the contract whose clauses they themselves wrote and ratified, yes, approved, justified, defended in another time but which, today, in our unsure hour, they declare they do not recognize or whose application they claim they never intended, they take to flight. Deluded creatures, they attempt withdrawal, 'tis some kind of mean protest they lamely seek to lodge when, poor idiots, they go into a voluntary retirement across the seas, wretched martyrs, saying, Why, it's totally beyond me, all this, you others had better make the best of it if it suits you, as for myself, I regret I can have no part in the thing, I'm a big man, there's no space for me in the dory, I've a furious sciatica, a lumbago, I'd not be able to pull an oar, I'm opposed, d'ye see, there's nothing for it, can't be of help, so won't stay, I feel in need of a change of air, of scene, 'tis got unpleasant here in these close quarters, adieu, and they dive. May they sink. Believe me, they usually do. Can this be the course you urge me to follow?

There is also another kind, just as bad, worse perhaps, and not very different. These are the ones who, equally selfish, lack the stuff to wash their hands and

be off to struggle with the tides and wind. No, they'll
not be shaken off, these drones: they are blind helms-
men and like nothing better than to drag their oar
or lose it overboard through no fault of their own,
mind you; nor is it their fault they need double rations.
They rock the boat they'd die rather than leave, they
live forever, retch exactly into the gale when one's
blowing, otherwise on their mates, have tender sto-
machs too, are always perishing of thirst, drop the
waterflask over the side, accuse who do not forgive
them at once, pretend distraction and piss on the
salt pork, weep for what they've done, then do more,
wax weary and fall asleep. Later, as from an hiber-
nation, they wake into a season and surrounding
radically unlike what they lastly remember or fondly
anticipate. While asleep, much is forgot, sleep im-
proves the universe, restores the sleeper; are these
not grubby knaves more deserving of scorn and ridi-
cule than blame and blows, who fancy all must stand
still while they nap? they are as freshborn babes that
open their blinking eyes and cry that we are lost. They
are bewildered; this, they say, is exceedingly queer,
how has it come to pass, why are we here? But no, a
sharp eye has scried land ahead; everyone strains at
the oars; 'tis a barren, stony isle, bleak and forbidding
they near. This will not do. They have nothing
but reproaches for the steadfast mariner who has
piloted his craft through God knows what storms and
seas and brought it within haven's reach at last. Ho!
they scoff, haw! exceedingly queer, very bitter indeed,
to have suffered so much, for so little. They sniff the
wind, analyze the shape of things over the bow. 'Tis
mighty unfamiliar, they bleat, where are we? Land?
But is it safe? do we dare? Or if the island is green

and friendly, have a peaceful and inviting aspect, 'tis then a mirage for fools, a waste of precious strength thus to press eagerly towards it. Astonishing and peculiar they find it, that men can be so heavily deceived; we are out of our senses, disordered; and if no mirage, but real, caution there, be careful, such places are defended by hidden reefs, fearsome currents and shallows, no, no, go back, better the sea than wrack, a stout heart, despair not. What an odious situation we are in, quoth the philosopher, and he yawns, he hunts for his biscuit and what's this? 'tis gone, stolen while he took his hard-earned rest! So there are bandits about, are there! whereanent sarcastic reflexions upon honor among thieves, the kind of common effort that can be made by common men, etc.

These buffoons—sometimes termed conservatives, sometimes liberals, but it's all one and the same—, these buffoons, I say, dispose of yet another subterfuge. They appeal to tradition in the prodigious belief that term is still the whip the people prefer to be flogged by: such-and-such a measure has no precedent, there is nothing in the past to sanction this manœuver, the test of time has not legitimated some other method; he has, this traditionalist, not the faintest interest in ends, or while he expounds the frightful doctrine of man as an end, the capital thing becomes the means, and what do you fancy are the means to a man all stomach, appetite and good taste? He is so much occupied with culture; he considers it his pleasurable duty endlessly to minister culture; he is always comparing, speaks of renaissance, reformation and of decadence, he reveres bygone days, abhors the present, has grave doubts about the future. He measures, he computes, shifts, thus passes his days in management, arranging transpositions, delightful effects, in establishing relationships, chatting with his accolytes, repairing the décor before which he supposes his subjectivity assumes fullness. Life, he argues, is only worth living within stable institutions; he has bought himself a castle or had one built; in it, he conducts his unclean revels, hears lectures, goes on with his owning, collecting, consolidating, is a convivial fellow, a figure of note; what would be a prison for an honest man is a paradise for this libertine. Ah, the question merits to be gone exhaustively into, for this species of villain, this sophist is adept, his vicious reasoning cannot be exploded too often. One has but to bend one's glance upon Aegillius and Sextus, return to the eight centuries after the Empire's subversion. Look to former days, these sly fellows advise us. And what is it we see? There are the decisions of 1228 to instruct us, or we may ponder 1231 when after a fifteen days' siege by a little band of Rhenish thugs, a council of seigneurs met and accounted the city beyond their means to defend. Vanity's wounds, the injuries to which Grön's amour-propre was submitted, they were all healed in time when at last it became evident a certain wisdom underlay what at first glance might be taken for feebleness. To understand is to forgive, they learned to say, and you may hear their posterity snigger it yet. To understand is to forgive, meanwhile raising one eyebrow, and thereafter, in age after age, mayors, generals, lords and cardinals sued for exemption, pled with skill and vigor and infrequent success: time and again the city was sacked, massacres succeeded massacres, each new experience outdid all former ones: yet Grön flourished, for, the scoundrels chorused, what arms can attain the spirit? Surveying the uninterrupted series of miscarriages, cementing a hundred calamities into a single grand disaster and reassured by the integral perfection of the design, a new dialectic introduced a new appreciation of the human sort—and aimed especially at enabling the ruined to put their sorrows out of mind. This peculiar, most subtle but, wonder of wonders! palatable idea was urged: that absolute destitution practically assured by unending misadventures is the mark whereby Providence distinguishes Its chosen: they only know the passion of hard times, the calvary of abandonment, reverses, sore travail for upon them alone are showered those inverse blessings which impart its value to the peace that passeth understanding, in none but them, they who are miserable, may hope be born. Regular defeat attested the city's virtue and thus its secret strength, such was the pernicious system. The speed and ease with which Grön could adopt an attitude of cringing and dread was the marvel of all Europe, and news of this fabulous, much abused but unattainted virgin, emblem of passivity, golden invitation, graciousness, generosity, reached even to the Oxus. The accepted plan—it became a habit, a national trait—, was planlessness; 'twas all imposture they had here; a simulacrum of faith, not steel, cuirassed and sinewed the city. With what regarded others, Grön exhibited resilience, remained on the move, tirelessly sank, fell, and when down, trembled, this with the greatest charm and sometimes piteous little sounds, a fluttering of the eyelids and reproachful but timid glances intended not to melt but rather to inflame the enemy. 'Twas the scheme to confound him by yielding to him instantly, with a semblance of joy, with allegresse before, indeed, he delivered the attack or the desire to deliver one was full arisen within him; to determine his desires, whet them, caress them; to provoke attack in order to be in a case to yield, to take up an helpless posture and put on an air of softness in order to favor the enemy's induration and encourage his illusion of strength, thuswise immediately to suggest an overwhelming disparity between his force and yours, to promote an intimacy that exhales lubricious tenderness; in this whorish fashion to stupify and exacerbate him till he is mad, till he surrenders himself to his effervescence; to excite lust, rage, regret in the enemy that the certainty, violence and favorable issue of his attack be ensured. That done, he is yours.

No, Aimée, no, little mother, we of this generation belong to no one; those luxuries are over, those couplings beseem us no longer. We have purified our national manners, in forty years we have accomplished miracles. We have banished artificial distinctions, integrated virtually every member of our society into a unity and learned to perceive and cope with individualism; the Republican mob has melted away, licence and egotism are rare with us, meaning has been restored to honor and fame and, like the Spartan warrior who, his shield dressed before him, saw in that polished mirror an image of the State, have recovered an idea of service and sacrifice and realized that we ourselves are the preferred aliment of what feeds us, and our blood the only liquor able to satisfy the high thirst of the power whereof in our turn we have souls that cry for drink. Today an austere and masculine people, what were we then? The fair target of the world's mockery and insult, ripe for any abuse, any bully's fag, a harlot to them all; we are now that same earth's scourge and terror: our look, the mere sight of us, has created a thousand neutrals; alone, self-sufficient, silent, we are the masterpiece of a system, a discipline, a faith. At the moment it is raining.

Today, Monday, the 6th of August, is Transfiguration; that might be worth noting; to tell the truth, it is hard to decide just what is worth noting, which details to offer, what to emphasize, what to suppress, for it is indifferent, it is indifferent. I woke this morning to find the sun up and smashing and Claude-Maxime our chief no longer and my paralyzed tongue unable to pose a multitude of questions. This afternoon Johnson was released, Father Shart, poor man, I should have adored giving his portrait, Father Shart was mistaken for someone else and stoned to death, Grimoald was shot, but surely that was to be expected. There have been hundreds of arrests and several major conflagrations, the St Andrä oil dumps are still afire. The rain, which began at three, is still coming down, mixed with smoke, a greasy black paint smearing everything, turning faces black and probably complicating the last identifications, for most of the heavy work was concluded by supper time. Yet, I dare say, it wasn't a very gay evening meal most of Grön's families ate. Woe is heavy here, the air is heavy and hot, we are in mourning and some of the firing squads are still working in the downpour, the brave fellows peering through the night, discharging volleys at scarcely visible eyes 'twould be superfluous to blindfold, and gravediggers scooping up mud with their shovels, or with their buckets, the brave fellows. Magnificent

people! this is your eulogy, there is not a man amongst
you who's not responded to the call. Leave Grön?
Desert them? Never; go if you like, Aimée, if you think
you can, but don't expect me to join you, I am destined
to end my days here, and I have known that a long
time.

Today, after my mid-day meal and our conference,
I left Petterade and Kuhl and went to walk with my
thoughts and think about the vital matters that would
so normally occupy a civil servant at such a moment:
would I be sacked? no, impossible; would I lose my
assistants? yes, in all likelihood, seven out of eight
would be dropped, even butchered. Would my salary
be cut, would rentals climb, would my insurance
premium be raised, would mortgage taxes mount,
would I be named to a civilian defense brigade, would
they halve our rations again? I followed the river for
a mile, crossed it, and came back along the other bank,
deeply immersed in conjecture, now pausing to look
at the slow stream, now glancing up at the darkening
sky, remembering the child I saw urinating early this
morning, wondering what the certain flood of heavenly
seed would create in the earth, wondering what I
would be on the earth, remembering your letter and
the other child, the dead one slain in the sunshine,
wondering whether this day were to be the last one,
whether it had been Marivaux', deciding that was
unlikely, discovering Johnson's name on my lips,
wondering whether it would not be far better to go and
find out what, if anything, lay in store for me. They
were executing scores of functionaries, indicators,
Clean Youths; they? why, my colleagues, the enquirers,
the national youth were on the job. I had concluded
that I ought to go at once to look for my name on the

lists; but one moment. Were there lists? Where were they posted? Had they been published already? Was it possible to compose and publish lists in six brief hours? Were they our old lists? in that case I would not find myself mentioned; but would I have to go back frequently? and if I had been overlooked, or my name misspelled? or my name usurped, or my number lost? I wanted to do the proper thing. They, I was sure, were doing the proper thing as proper they saw it in the frenzy and muddle. Be cool, I told myself, be cool, old man, even if they have falsified your identity. A strange sight cooled me: I had come to the Aegillian Bridge, on the south bank opposite the Place des Philosophes: there, gathered about a lamp-post, was a group of roughly fifty persons, half in uniform, the other half townsmen. Officers were shouting orders, political leaders were shouting orders: the object of their attentions was a man who had been almost entirely deprived of his identity. One party was busily hanging him, the other cutting him down with pocket-knives, short axes and little scythes; up he would go, down he would come, up again, down again; the noose would be fitted around his bleeding neck and zip! he would rise, the knives, the axes, the scythes would be brought into play, would slash at clothing, legs, rope and zip! he would descend. Blood spouted from a gashed knee, oozed from an almost broken and thoroughly peeled neck; what was to be this man's fate? would he live? would he die? was he alive, was he dead? one cannot always tell upon the basis of a first impression, or a second, such matters are not to be judged in haste, was he to be spared, as seemed to feel obligatory those who were hewing and hacking him to pieces, or to be despatched, as strongly appeared to be the view of the other faction, some of whose adherents, whether more or less convinced of what required to be done, were springing into the air and clinging to their prize, while he dangled in the air... but to reclaim him? drag him back to earth safe and sound? or to assure his strangulation? Why, all these are silly questions, aren't they, perfectly useless, I suppose so, for you know what happened, oh I dare say you do: he who most loudly advocated saving this ruin, finally gaining his way, seized up a scythe and with a fine stout motion cut its neck four-fifths through; at the same moment, the rope parted, the corpse fell, a soldier landed on top of it, stunned or intrigued or petrified by that full-length, mouth-to-mouth, groin-to-groin, knee-to-knee man-to-man contact, lay staring at the enormous worried eyes of the deceased. They had to apply force to pry the young man away from the body and I saw him sobbing and shaking and wriggling, his underlip quivering, gritting his teeth, ashamed but weeping all the same, as if his heart were broken. That must have been an experience he will remember. For such spectacles are touching, aren't they? I shall always be moved by them. A person walking about Grön had the opportunity this afternoon to witness scores. But, on the other hand, had the succession proceeded smoothly, had the Objector taken the reins without incident, without certain preliminaries, excisions, gestures, Draconian proclamations, he would not have been worthy of the great man who designated him his heir. Yes, broadly speaking, matters seemed to be rather well in hand; this was reassuring to one who knew what was at stake, and I resumed my stroll.

A litttle while ago I believe I mentioned that everything is in serene equilibrium; the thought, the con-

viction came to me as I sauntered towards home,
passed the eleventh precinct police commissariat
whence, as from the adjoining abattoir the authorities
requisitioned a year or two ago and transformed into
an annex, came sounds of activity, sharp, poignant
sounds, individually disagreeable to the ear, collectively
melodious; the thought, I say, occurred to me that
the more various, multiple and discordant the manifestations of divine balance, the more firmly it is established, the more surely the mechanism runs. Matter
enters different forms and departs them, but the forms
endure, so does the substance; there is naught real,
naught distrainable, naught meaningful but this movement, but this incessation, but this naught, but the
eternal recurrence of things; all that is, goes, all goes,
and going, goes well, save for one thing. For one
thing only.

And here a younger man, a man less weary, sounder,
more sanguine, at this point another, a younger Lucius
would perhaps hesitate before that mysterious *one thing
only*, retreat before it if he understood it, or, most likely
of all, not understand it : ignorance or dread of it is
what permits young Lucius to be young.

That thing, although an illusion, possesses a voice.
It touches our nerves, intends our vitals, infects our
dreams, wrecks our peace. It is a certain spirit of
perversity that darts poisoned arrows into what is sure
and sound, that maims and puts the look of caricature
upon what is whole and authentic. It is the abominable irrelevance, the disease, the sign of trouble, the
source of confusion, Nature's error, the unique flaw,
the infamy that can only have been invented that the
ultimate honor be decreed him who were to crush it,
and yet, my friend, it's not been crushed, all inclines

to its obliteration, but its sinister hand is very strong, it goes abroad in night's time and the evil season, it finds out lonely men and speaks cunningly to them, steals rotbearing into their hearts like the first bane, puts fury and ice there and makes them mad. The horror of the universe, it is what calls the universe horrid and makes the universe believe it, it is blame and guile, the curling finger, the bent regard, the soft bent back. It is Philoctetes defiling the sacred isle and persecuting the sun. It is the defeat of enterprise, the rout of reason, the appalling thorn, the vineyard beast, the grape's rot. Ah, wed continents, go drain seas, fashion deserts, level mountains, break the planet out of shape and course, yes, do that so as to learn this world must be annihilated that the curse be stifled, the inextirpable weed consumed... and even then? Criminal, disruptive principle, thou hast wrestled with immensity, thou hast killed stars with thy lethal puissance, hast burst galaxies by sounding thy ambitions; and indeed, my dear, I, a very ordinary man, I sometimes think that if nebulae enlarge, if what space holds is rushing away from us, it is because of some supreme loathing things do retire from what a human grimace represents... I spied it surely in the face of the man they had hanged. I see it plainly now. But after they had thrown the hanged man into the river I could not go on; I turned on my heel and dashed back to the police commissariat. My hand shaking, I wrote out an application for a gun. I am entitled to have one; they issued me a pistol and six cartridges. It was then the first drops of rain began to fall through the stifling air; why, the rain did not quite fall, it was expelled, as if squeezed through a sieve by the weight of the dense clouds of smoke hanging in front of the sun, a russet scorch or stain. The rain, fine and quick, came like a mist of oily ink. I began to cough. I was filthy by the time I reached home.

The proper thing, the only thing was to cleanse myself immediately. I began to peel off my clothing; "Draw me a bath, hurry," I called; nothing answered my nakedness. I remembered that Marivaux had walked out upon me, leaving me in a ridiculous and prejudicial position. I cursed the dog. The room was dark; waiting, my body felt both huge and incredibly small. I was beyond words depressed. I clawed at the electric light switch; nothing happened, I tried another; the current was dead. "Then get that damned bath started!" I shouted; once again it seemed the vainest formality to realize that I was alone, that I had made a mistake. I saw nothing amusing in it. However, I thought I might laugh and, producing a heaving within my breast, may have laughed, although I heard nothing. The convulsion continued or changed itself into shivering: hot as it was (I supposed it was hot; I had been in a fierce sweat) my moist flesh felt sheathed in a film of ice. I thrashed about, came upon my suit-coat, donned it askew, tore it off in a panic, ripping the lining and dislodging the pistol, which bounded to the floor, striking my bare foot. I cried out in pain, once. In a rage (the gun had not gone off), I kicked the pistol, and cried out again. Twisting my mouth, blinking my eyes, I looked down, my chin on my chest, and explored my body with my hands: they descended my breasts, my ribs, my belly and converged at my groin. The idea of Marivaux' perfidy exasperated me. I sought to calm myself; the effort exhausted me. I had absolutely to have light. The trip to the kitchen was difficult and prolonged. Laboriously, I made my way back to the living room, to before the fireplace, clutching a box of matches in one hand, a soft pliant candle in the other; having waited this long, I decided to delay striking the match: I stood still, a draught of air swept down the chimney, tortured my legs from thigh to ankle. I was prepared for what the flame revealed. Can you still visualize me as a young man? Has your brain's grip upon that happy image never weakened? Have you cherished that memory, has it been your sweetest consolation, my dear? Well, bless your heart! I lovingly studied that extraordinary visage, I placed the candle in a hundred various positions, exploited every possibility, adjusting each feature, arranging and then rumpling my hair, grinning, frowning, distorting my nose and mouth with my fingers, putting out my tongue, drawing back or pinching or kneading my soiled skin. I could think of nothing but the night we had come upon Johnson in the toilet twenty-eight years ago. He was out now. What was he like? Was he reformed, that is to say, had he yielded up his form? or was he still calm, still admirable in his self-sufficiency, had he yet his gravity, was his proud decorum unimpaired or had it undone him? What would he do now? Would he become an advisor, or a leader? or be kept in reserve, sent back to mature in his cell? Where else could he go? He had no apartment, no papers, no birds, no money, his health might be poor, his spirit alienated, to whom could he turn? What, I wondered, if he were to arrive at my home? Would he enter my house abruptly, penetrate rudely in, surprise me? What would he say upon seeing me? He would, I concluded, say nothing, thank God no, for he was totally blind, so at least someone had informed

me, and it was not unlikely, he had himself predicted
it; hence, he would speak, if he were to speak at all,
in darkness, unseeingly, to me; or not to me, for was
I known to him? we had never been introduced; would
he know where he was were he to enter here, would
I not have to tell him as I took his white cane from
his hand? but would I be able to? would he surrender
his stick as readily as that? He was not familiar with
my voice and had no reason to accept my word for
anything whatsoever, above all because he was blind,
no doubt of his blindness existed in my mind, and
the blind, more sensitive than we to sound, to dis-
cerning vibrations, the conditions, the motives that
produce sound, are perfectly capable of perceiving in-
sincerity, the softest note of treachery in a word. In
the bathroom I found that the water had been turned off.

Hours passed. You can be sure of that. No, I
declared, not an ace of doubt. The man has now lost
the use of his other eye. Would he come wearing
two patches? Would they be of expensive silk, as
before? Or tinted glasses? Has that second eye been
extracted? Might he have been reduced to wadding
cotton into the socket? And what today are one's
chances of replacing old dirty cotton with new? I
imagined he would be needy, it occured to me that,
suddenly cast adrift, he would perhaps be compelled
to beg, for a while, until he had got his bearings, perhaps permanently; the hope of finding a crust of bread
might lead him to me, pure luck, that is to say, might
put him in my hands. I rather hoped it would not
be thus, for I had no bread to give him, I was myself
hungry, I had to be careful lest hunger plunge me
into doing things I would regret instantly; this Johnson

had a notoriously fine palate. I placed kindling
and a few short logs in the fireplace, lit a fire, drew up
a chair, and folded my hands. I was still naked for
it seemed to me best that way to be in the event I had
visitors, and I had strong hopes some, or preferably
one, would call upon me. I had the intimation it was
now or never, I was ready for virtually any visitor
or event, spiritually prepared through hope. Yes,
I have done a considerable amount of hoping during
my otherwise not very active lifetime, just about as
much hoping as could be fitted into a lifetime of waiting, waiting, if you follow me, not primarily for something to arrive, but rather waiting for now or never to
dawn, a liberating, integrating recognition that would
surely be... Not that I needed company; it seemed
to me that this was the moment par excellence to try
to have it. Hence, I assumed the attitude: drew up
my knees, lowered them, straining my feet so that the
toes barely touched the floor; my abdominal muscles
grew taut, I inhaled and held my breath, dug my
fingernails into my palms, bent my swimming head,
half-closed my swollen eyes, and pushed to move the
world. The fire crackled on the hearth.

Ah, my dear, what a picture of determination and of
expectancy, of trust, of dolour! I summoned all my
powers to the effort, my resolution was strengthened
by a review of all that had passed on this crucial
Monday. In the course of my early morning pro-
menade signs advise me of impending trouble; word
of the Accuser's death reaches me before I am able
to begin breakfast. Breakfast over, I suddenly receive
a communication from you, a relic from the past.
Though I do not read it at once, it has all the same
a potent effect upon me. It is a warning as much

as a reminder: I am stirred, moved to interrogate myself, to open wide my eyes and look about me. Circumstances put an end to the relationship between my man-servant and me and an ancient thorn is drawn from my side. But the wounds bleed afresh, I suffer much, the pain is redoubled by the efforts that must be made ere the flesh is mended. Dazed, numbed, I venture abroad. I see a child immolated before my intendent eyes which a few hours previously saw another child design the end of everything; two rituals, each of heavy significance, before lunch; I am somewhat soothed. For however much death affrights, it also shocks, and it is shock I await, to be cured, absolved, purged. While doom echoes round the place, a slaughter is made; a therapeutic vision, the end of the world! My appetite is restored, I am a man again. General Kuhl and Colonel Petterade and I dine simply, frugally, mainly on liquids. Meanwhile, a devouring war rages in its forty-ninth year and I sit in the presence of its apotheosis, that prodigious military virtue that everlastingly accrues, dilates, gains upon its adversary.

For of the two universal principles, pure good is in the ascendant. Enchanted, I watch the endless surge and ebbing in our human affairs, I am witness to the rhythmic, the immense peristalsis, and I ask, when will this His wrathful will be done? When will the fight be over? When will history be made? The angry little sphere of shit, oh when will God be rid of it? When will this patience be rewarded? this confidence vindicated? how much longer must salvation be present in the waiting? How much longer must this widowhood continue? When will strike the hour of union, the annunciatory burst of wind, when will it break? When, you ask, when will this solitude and desolation end, this perpetual fall reach its term? Never? Or are we there, Aimée? Or nearly? Now, Aimée, is this the time, or may not this time be as good as any other, and suffice? Is that Johnson stamping and swearing in the blackness, is that his touch on the latch, his weight invading my doubts? And is this truly a gun's barrel, can this truly be a gun I am sucking, licking the oil from the bore? And is this a true stink of nitre assaults my nose, and fire scratching in my eye?

He did not seem the large man, the imposing man I had imagined him.

How ashamed I was as I stiffened, ashamed even as I insulted him, luxuriously ashamed as, starting back, he raised his white cane and his white face; I snatched a burning stick from the fire, flung it at his blind cheek: I taunted him, I screamed at him, cursed him, menaced him, bade him be a man and strike me if he dared, swore I'd kill him if he did not. I showed him what I meant, I guided his arm; cringing, I slapped his face to heat him, I laughed, I implored him to rouse me, I explained that I simply could never discipline myself, I was ashamed, he beat me, and I was happy. I wept from pleasure; laughing, choking, I slid down and lay in my filth. I lay in my filth, wriggling, smiling, wondering.

Then after a while he too sat down, wearily, and remained there in his shrunken bulk brooding and thinking his own thoughts; I watched him until I lost all interest in him, until he no longer meant anything to me, nor represented any further possibility.

Paris, 1953.

PETROS ABATZOGLOU, *What Does Mrs. Freeman Want?*

PIERRE ALBERT-BIROT, *Grabinoulor*

YUZ ALESHKOVSKY, *Kangaroo*

FELIPE ALFAU, *Chromos* • *Locos*

IVAN ÂNGELO, *The Celebration* • *The Tower of Glass*

DAVID ANTIN, *Talking*

DJUNA BARNES, *Ladies Almanack* • *Ryder*

JOHN BARTH, *LETTERS* • *Sabbatical*

DONALD BARTHELME, *The King* • *Paradise*

SVETISLAV BASARA, *Chinese Letter*

MARK BINELLI, *Sacco and Vanzetti Must Die!*

ANDREI BITOV, *Pushkin House.*

LOUIS PAUL BOON, *Chapel Road* • *Summer in Termuren*

ROGER BOYLAN, *Killoyle*

IGNÁCIO DE LOYOLA BRANDÃO, *Teeth under the Sun* • *Zero*

CHRISTINE BROOKE-ROSE, *Amalgamemnon*

BRIGID BROPHY, *In Transit*

MEREDITH BROSNAN, *Mr. Dynamite*

GERALD L. BRUNS, *Modern Poetry and the Idea of Language*

GABRIELLE BURTON, *Heartbreak Hotel*

MICHEL BUTOR, *Degrees* • *Mobile* • *Portrait of the Artist as a Young Ape*

G. CABRERA INFANTE, *Infante's Inferno* • *Three Trapped Tigers*

JULIETA CAMPOS, *The Fear of Losing Eurydice*

ANNE CARSON, *Eros the Bittersweet*

CAMILO JOSÉ CELA, *The Family of Pascual Duarte* • *The Hive.* • *Christ versus Arizona*

LOUIS-FERDINAND CÉLINE, *Castle to Castle* • *Conversations with Professor Y* • *London Bridge* • *North* • *Rigadoon*

HUGO CHARTERIS, *The Tide Is Right*

JEROME CHARYN, *The Tar Baby*

MARC CHOLODENKO, *Mordechai Schamz*

EMILY HOLMES COLEMAN, *The Shutter of Snow*

ROBERT COOVER, *A Night at the Movies*

STANLEY CRAWFORD, *Some Instructions to My Wife*

ROBERT CREELEY, *Collected Prose*

RENÉ CREVEL, *Putting My Foot in It*

RALPH CUSACK, *Cadenza*

SUSAN DAITCH, *L.C.* • *Storytown*

NIGEL DENNIS, *Cards of Identity*

PETER DIMOCK, *A Short Rhetoric for Leaving the Family*

ARIEL DORFMAN, *Konfidenz*

COLEMAN DOWELL, *The Houses of Children* • *Island People* • *Too Much Flesh and Jabez*

RIKKI DUCORNET, *The Complete Butcher's Tales* • *The Fountains of Neptune* • *The Jade Cabinet* • *Phosphor in Dreamland* • *The Stain* • *The Word "Desire."*

WILLIAM EASTLAKE, *The Bamboo Bed* • *Castle Keep* • *Lyric of the Circle Heart*

JEAN ECHENOZ, *Chopin's Move*

STANLEY ELKIN, *A Bad Man* • *Boswell: A Modern Comedy* • *Criers and Kibitzers, Kibitzers and Criers* • *The Dick Gibson Show* • *The Franchiser* • *George Mills* • *The Living End* • *The MacGuffin* • *The Magic Kingdom* • *Mrs.*

Ted Bliss • *The Rabbi of Lud* • *Van Gogh's Room at Arles*

ANNIE ERNAUX, *Cleaned Out*

LAUREN FAIRBANKS, *Muzzle Thyself* • *Sister Carrie*

LESLIE A. FIEDLER, *Love and Death in the American Novel*

GUSTAVE FLAUBERT, *Bouvard and Pécuchet*

FORD MADOX FORD, *The March of Literature*

JON FOSSE, *Melancholy*

MAX FRISCH, *I'm Not Stiller* • *Man in the Holocene*

CARLOS FUENTES, *Christopher Unborn* • *Distant Relations* • *Terra Nostra* • *Where the Air Is Clear*

JANICE GALLOWAY, *Foreign Parts* • *The Trick Is to Keep Breathing*

WILLIAM H. GASS, *The Tunnel* • *Willie Masters' Lonesome Wife*

ETIENNE GILSON, *The Arts of the Beautiful* • *Forms and Substances in the Arts*

C. S. GISCOMBE, *Giscome Road* • *Here*

DOUGLAS GLOVER, *Bad News of the Heart* • *The Enamoured Knight*

KAREN ELIZABETH GORDON, *The Red Shoes*

GEORGI GOSPODINOV, *Natural Novel*

JUAN GOYTISOLO, *Marks of Identity*

PATRICK GRAINVILLE, *The Cave of Heaven*

HENRY GREEN, *Blindness* • *Concluding* • *Doting* • *Nothing*

JIŘÍ GRUŠA, *The Questionnaire*

JOHN HAWKES, *Whistlejacket*

AIDAN HIGGINS, *A Bestiary* • *Bornholm Night-Ferry* • *Flotsam and Jetsam* • *Langrishe, Go Down* • *Scenes from a Receding Past* • *Windy Arbours*

ALDOUS HUXLEY, *Antic Hay* • *Crome Yellow* • *Point Counter Point* • *Those Barren Leaves* • *Time Must Have a Stop*

MIKHAIL IOSSEL AND JEFF PARKER, EDS., *Amerika: Contemporary Russians View the United States*

GERT JONKE, *Geometric Regional Novel*

JACQUES JOUET, *Mountain R*

HUGH KENNER, *The Counterfeiters* • *Flaubert, Joyce and Beckett: The Stoic Comedians* • *Joyce's Voices*

DANILO KIŠ, *Garden, Ashes* • *A Tomb for Boris Davidovich*

ANITA KONKKA, *A Fool's Paradise*

GEORGE KONRÁD, *The City Builder*

TADEUSZ KONWICKI, *A Minor Apocalypse* • *The Polish Complex*

MENIS KOUMANDAREAS, *Koula*

ELAINE KRAF, *The Princess of 72nd Street*

JIM KRUSOE, *Iceland*

EWA KURYLUK, *Century 21*

VIOLETTE LEDUC, *La Bâtarde*

DEBORAH LEVY, *Billy and Girl* • *Pillow Talk in Europe and Other Places*

JOSÉ LEZAMA LIMA, *Paradiso*

ROSA LIKSOM, *Dark Paradise*

OSMAN LINS, *Avalovara* • *The Queen of the Prisons of Greece*

ALF MAC LOCHLAINN, *The Corpus in the Library* • *Out of Focus*

RON LOEWINSOHN, *Magnetic Field(s)*

FOR A FULL LIST OF PUBLICATIONS, VISIT:
www.dalkeyarchive.com

D. Keith Mano, *Take Five*
Ben Marcus, *The Age of Wire and String*
Wallace Markfield, *Teitlebaum's Window.* • *To an Early Grave*
David Markson, *Reader's Block* • *Springer's Progress* • *Wittgenstein's Mistress*
Carole Maso, *AVA*
Ladislav Matejka and Krystyna Pomorska, eds., *Readings in Russian Poetics: Formalist and Structuralist Views*
Harry Mathews, *The Case of the Persevering Maltese: Collected Essays* • *Cigarettes* • *The Conversions* • *The Human Country: New and Collected Stories* • *The Journalist* • *My Life in CIA* • *Singular Pleasures* • *The Sinking of the Odradek Stadium* • *Tlooth* • *20 Lines a Day*
Robert L. McLaughlin, ed., *Innovations: An Anthology of Modern & Contemporary Fiction*
Herman Melville, *The Confidence-Man*
Steven Millhauser, *The Barnum Museum* • *In the Penny Arcade*
Ralph J. Mills, Jr., *Essays on Poetry.*
Olive Moore, *Spleen.*
Nicholas Mosley, *Accident.* • *Assassins.* • *Catastrophe Practice.* • *Children of Darkness and Light* • *Experience and Religion* • *The Hesperides Tree* • *Hopeful Monsters* • *Imago Bird* • *Impossible Object* • *Inventing God* • *Judith* • *Look at the Dark.* • *Natalie Natalia* • *Serpent* • *Time at War* • *The Uses of Slime Mould: Essays of Four Decades*
Warren F. Motte, Jr., *Fables of the Novel: French Fiction since 1990* • *Oulipo: A Primer of Potential Literature*
Yves Navarre, *Our Share of Time* • *Sweet Tooth*
Dorothy Nelson, *In Night's City* • *Tar and Feathers*
Wilfrido D. Nolledo, *But for the Lovers*
Flann O'Brien, *At Swim-Two-Birds* • *At War* • *The Best of Myles* • *The Dalkey Archive* • *Further Cuttings* • *The Hard Life* • *The Poor Mouth* • *The Third Policeman*
Claude Ollier, *The Mise-en-Scène*
Patrik Ouředník, *Europeana*
Fernando del Paso, *Palinuro of Mexico*
Robert Pinget, *The Inquisitory* • *Mahu or The Material* • *Trio*
Raymond Queneau, *The Last Days* • *Odile* • *Pierrot Mon Ami* • *Saint Glinglin*
Ann Quin, *Berg* • *Passages* • *Three* • *Tripticks*
Ishmael Reed, *The Free-Lance Pallbearers* • *The Last Days of Louisiana Red* • *Reckless Eyeballing* • *The Terrible Three.* • *The Terrible Twos* • *Yellow Back Radio Broke-Down*
Julián Ríos, *Larva: A Midsummer Night's Babel* • *Poundemonium*
Augusto Roa Bastos, *I the Supreme*
Jacques Roubaud, *The Great Fire of London* • *Hortense in Exile* • *Hortense Is Abducted* • *The Plurality of Worlds of Lewis* • *The Princess Hoppy* • *The Form of a City*

Changes Faster, Alas, Than the Human Heart • *Some Thing Black*
Leon S. Roudiez, *French Fiction Revisited*
Vedrana Rudan, *Night*
Lydie Salvayre, *The Company of Ghosts* • *Everyday Life* • *The Lecture*
Luis Rafael Sánchez, *Macho Camacho's Beat*
Severo Sarduy, *Cobra & Maitreya*
Nathalie Sarraute, *Do You Hear Them?* • *Martereau* • *The Planetarium*
Arno Schmidt, *Collected Stories* • *Nobodaddy's Children*
Christine Schutt, *Nightwork*
Gail Scott, *My Paris*
June Akers Seese, *Is This What Other Women Feel Too?* • *What Waiting Really Means*
Aurelie Sheehan, *Jack Kerouac Is Pregnant*
Viktor Shklovsky, *Knight's Move* • *A Sentimental Journey: Memoirs 1917-1922* • *Energy of Delusion: A Book on Plot* • *Theory of Prose* • *Third Factory* • *Zoo, or Letters Not about Love*
Josef Škvorecký, *The Engineer of Human Souls*
Claude Simon, *The Invitation*
Gilbert Sorrentino, *Aberration of Starlight* • *Blue Pastoral* • *Crystal Vision* • *Imaginative Qualities of Actual Things* • *Mulligan Stew* • *Pack of Lies* • *Red the Fiend* • *The Sky Changes* • *Something Said* • *Splendide-Hôtel* • *Steelwork* • *Under the Shadow*
W. M. Spackman, *The Complete Fiction*
Gertrude Stein, *Lucy Church Amiably* • *The Making of Americans* • *A Novel of Thank You*
Piotr Szewc, *Annihilation*
Stefan Themerson, *Hobson's Island* • *The Mystery of the Sardine* • *Tom Harris*
Jean-Philippe Toussaint, *Television*
Dumitru Tsepeneag, *Vain Art of the Fugue*
Esther Tusquets, *Stranded*
Dubravka Ugresic, *Lend Me Your Character* • *Thank You for Not Reading*
Mati Unt, *Things in the Night*
Eloy Urroz, *The Obstacles*
Luisa Valenzuela, *He Who Searches*
Boris Vian, *Heartsnaatcher*
Austryn Wainhouse, *Hedyphagetica*
Paul West, *Words for a Deaf Daughter & Gala*
Curtis White, *America's Magic Mountain* • *The Idea of Home* • *Memories of My Father Watching TV* • *Monstrous Possibility: An Invitation to Literary* • *Politics* • *Requiem*
Diane Williams, *Excitability: Selected Stories* • *Romancer Erector.*
Douglas Woolf, *Wall to Wall* • *Ya! & John-Juan*
Philip Wylie, *Generation of Vipers*
Marguerite Young, *Angel in the Forest* • *Miss MacIntosh, My Darling*
ReYoung, *Unbabbling*
Zoran Živković, *Hidden Camera*
Louis Zukofsky, *Collected Fiction.*
Scott Zwiren, *God Head*

FOR A FULL LIST OF PUBLICATIONS, VISIT:
www.dalkeyarchive.com